# MIAMI
# REVELATIONS

## A STRUGGLE TO STAY ALIVE

*Victoria Hamilton Lauziere*

Publisher, Copyright, and Additional Information

*Miami Revelations* by Victoria Hamilton Lauziere

ISBN- 978-1-737-8338-0-2

Editing by Michael Sandlin
Cover design and interior design by Rafael Andres

*Dedication*

*This book is dedicated to my parents.
To my Mom, Dorothy Hamilton, who pulled me back when
I walked on the edge. To my Dad, my hero, Denzil Hamilton, who taught me to reach to the stars and realize my
dreams. When I felt scared or defeated his positive motivation gave me strength to succeed. I miss them so much!*

*To my sister, Sherri Hamilton Smith, who is my lifelong
sidekick. I love her for being with me through all our many
adventures, wreaking havoc on boys who could not tell us
apart!*

*And most of all to my husband Ken Lauziere, who never
doubts my decisions and joins me in my crazy endeavors
without hesitation. He always remembers the first thing I
said to him when he jumped into the car, "Buckle up baby
and get ready for the time of your life!"*

## Acknowledgements

A big thank you to Jose Trueba, who read my last draft to ensure the credibility. Jose moved into the house next door with his family after his father Domingo Trueba, a valiant man who left his family in Miami to fight for his Cuba, losing his life during the Bay of Pigs.

I also want to thank Diane Ludlam Suchy, who I met in first grade as we traveled through high school in Miami. Diane was the only one who asked me if she could read my first draft, taking it to a printer to read it carefully, and edit it using her keen intelligence.

Most of all, Maria Pease, my college professor and author of the Sam Parker Mystery Series, Malicious Intent, Malicious Secrets, and Malicious Desires. Maria Pease encouraged and guided me every step of the way, to finish my book!

# CHAPTER 1

"Hey, Dad, I'm going to be a hooker," is not something every father dreams of hearing. I was leaving the house for my new assignment. The spandex skirt and low-cut tank top were a dead giveaway. But in my case, it came as a blessing. Dad knew that I had to do whatever it took to get the job done. Even so, the uniform was a bitch.

It is 1985, and the center of Miami is a swamp and not the kind where gators, mosquitoes, and snakes are found. This is the Miami of Scarface's reign after all the prisoners and miscreants from Castro's boatlift became wards of Florida, giving new meaning to the words *naturally terrifying*. It is the era of *Miami Vice*, but the pastels and fast cars were only for those who had connections. The rest were just desperate drug addicts, thugs, arsonists, and prostitutes.

I could see my partner, Mercedes, on the corner a few blocks ahead. The neon and fluorescent lights reflected on her sweaty skin—she was showing a lot of that skin. Mercedes was an exotic Cuban beauty and was not happy being a lady of the night. I was running late, and I could tell she was pissed off. It was not my fault. I knew full well how dangerous this part of town was. Carlos was my ride, and he had to borrow a friend's car just to drop me off. There was no way he would drive his white Z28 Camaro with the flashy orange flames into this part of town. He would be lucky to escape with the air from his tires. His buddy's loaner was a clunky Honda hatchback held together by primer paint.

"Stop here," I said. "She's three blocks away, you'll be flat on your face before you get to the corner," he argued.

"I can walk three blocks." "Baby, it's not you I doubt, it's those pimp stilts... I don't want you to mess them up." He could not help but laugh at the idea that I might wear this ridiculous getup for him. Even though we were not dating anymore, he was one protective Cuban.

I smacked him and announced myself to the 'hood with an ear-splitting screech from the rusty door as it opened. I tottered across four lanes of asphalt; the heel of my right stiletto got stuck with every other step. Miami is so hot. I do not think the asphalt ever fully hardens. I am pigeon-toed, so my right leg comes down harder when I walk. And, in this butt-hugging outfit, the left side of my skirt rode up every time my left leg moved. *Thunk* went the right, *click* went the left, and then I would yank down the skirt. *Thunk, click, yank, thunk, click, yank...*

I knew Carlos was watching every step because I did not hear the Honda chug away. Imagining him watching me while laughing his ass off made me laugh so hard I made it across despite my handicap. While making my way down the sidewalk toward Mercedes, I heard the hatchback sputter by.

"Hey, Lady, how much for a ride?" Carlos shouted out the window.

"Come back when you can afford a real car," I shouted and did not even look at him. *Thunk, click, yank.* I passed burnt-out shops homeless vagrants.

Gangbangers ogled me. A shopkeeper pulled down his iron gate for the night. "Your kind is not welcome here," he hissed.

I kept my sights on Mercedes but realized it was a mistake to wear the bleached blonde wig against my Wonder Bread white skin; my hair was naturally blonde, but then none of these gals paraded around in their real hair. I was like a beacon of misguided light on the dark side of the tracks. I just reminded myself that it came with the job and marched on… *Thunk, click, yank.*

"You're late, Roni. I know it's cool to be hot, but I'm melting my falsies off," Mercedes said.

I was used to Mercedes's pointed dramatics, so I knew it was just her way of saying, "Good to see you." I sort of felt bad for her because she was darker. She fit in around here. Mercedes had skin that bronzed in the Miami broiler, and I had skin that blistered. If it were not for her genuinely bubbly personality this could have been her permanent corner.

I picked at my right heel tip where the rubber met the road and decided it could stay. I had to survive with a nail as a heel tip or go barefoot. A thug whistled at me through his gold-tipped teeth, and for a second, I felt like smashing them out with my nail heel but that would have ruined the work I desperately needed to do.

"It's not the heat, Mer. It is the humanity. "

"Ain't that the truth."

As I wedged my swollen right foot back into the impossible shoe, I lost my balance while yanking my skirt down. Mercedes caught me, and I started cracking up. It was the sort of laugh that comes out through your eyes and runs down your cheeks.

"I guess if I really want to score tonight, I need to stop yanking my skirt down," I managed to say during my thirty-seconds of lucidity between laughs.

"You're all class," Mercedes said.

Wiping my eyes, I caught a whiff of something burning. It was the smell of heat. Have you ever seen a movie where they show a lone figure on the desert horizon and the air seems to quaver in heat? Mix that visual with the blast of opening an oven door baking wood, metal, and cement, and that is the scent of an urban inferno.

"I'm guessing it's a different kind of joint on fire," Mercedes said as she caught a glimpse of my nose in the air.

Her answer came as sirens tore through like bullet trains speeding along uneven tracks. I sprang to attention and waited for the first engine to pass. As it neared, the reprobates of the hood did not flinch, but they did make themselves scarce. To say they were like cockroaches under the sudden flick of a light is probably unfair, but then again, the night was young.

Mercedes and I stood our ground inside the cone of reverberating angst that fire engines emit as they race by with sirens blaring and lights glaring. There was not much concern for windows breaking, as most had already been smashed around here. The smart shops had their windows caged and were closed for the night. My concern was with the fire trucks—more specifically what station they were from. My swollen ankles nearly gave in as I got my answer.

"Fourteen, shit!" I kicked off those nasty-ass heels and sprinted to keep up with the trucks. Suddenly my skirt hiking up was an advantage, my legs pumped like those of a nubile fifteen-year-old trying out for the track team. I know this because the lowlifes who lined the streets could care less about the fire trucks; they were more interested in the lily-white flesh bouncing past them.

The trucks turned the corner, and I got a chance to close the distance. But in batting off the multiethnic ass grabs coming at me, my gain was short lived. I turned the corner gasping, pulling breath from my throbbing lungs. I halted facing a wall of fire. It was a ten-story apartment building to be precise. It was situated in such a way that it consumed the entire width of the block like the Gates of Hell.

To face an inferno is one of the most surreal feelings a person can experience. Being consumed by lava is far removed and rare to a girl from Miami or Anywhere, USA. We go through life never thinking the ground we stand on can engulf us. Even Florida's frequent hurricanes descend from the sky with fair warning. A fire this big feeds off everything within reach: the air, the buildings, the ground, the people. Everything becomes like that warbled vision then flashover.

Police cars soon blared their way in-between to create a barrier to prevent me and other onlookers from going any closer to the fire.

Tears ran down my face as the smoke thickened, but I did not dare look away. I had to make sure he was not doing anything foolish. I already knew he was a hero—*why, why*, did he have to prove it on a daily basis? I searched everywhere, and the only person I connected with was... Mario? Are you shitting me? Mario Morales? He was no-good when he was twelve, fresh off the boat from Cuba. His presence at the fire scene made my stomach churn. I could not pinpoint why. I knew the feeling would bite me in the ass later as it submerged deep in the pit of my stomach. I stepped toward him when Mercedes caught up and handed me my shoes, saved again by her good timing. Partners, perfectly matched, can be difference between life and death.

"When did Miami become a place where you need shoes?" I muttered. My brain was melting. I stomped barefoot toward the first engine. Ouch! My flesh burned as I stopped to put on my shoes. An officer just getting out of his response vehicle tried to stop me, but I was undeterred. Ripping their masks off too early, choking from the toxic fumes, four firefighters burst from the doors of the crumbling building. "Come on, where are you?"

The lead firefighter lifted his headgear and shouted, "Get the airbag, Captain's got a little girl!"

'*Captain,*' my boiling mind thought, '*he's still in there.*' The fire sucked the water and air from my body. I was that lone figure on the deserted desert highway raging from the inside out in an all-consuming heat. The next minute or two happened all at once in Hell's melting pot. No wonder they named Miami's NBA team the *Miami Heat!*

The crew inflated a giant blue rescue air bag. A window popped and crashed down from above. "Daddy!" I screamed.

From the window, the captain of Station 14 tossed a little girl. Her body wafted toward the blue air bag, but I could not watch. My only interest was the captain, my dad. My body was so sapped of fluid that I could not even keep my eyes wet enough to focus. As I stared through my molten-dry eyes at the smashed window, the roof of the blazing building collapsed. The captain raised his arms and made a shadow puppet like he always did for my sister Sheila and I—his hands the wings of a poetic wave. For a split second, there were no sirens, no deafening flames, no suffocating smoke. It was just the shadow puppet and I—saying goodbye.

In the next second, my mournful screams surpassed all the sirens in Miami. It was 1985, and me, thirty-four-year-old Veronica Hamilton, just witnessed her hero burning to death, and all I could think about was that if he did see me, if he was sending me that poetic wave goodbye, his last vision of me was that of a prostitute. That is not an image any daughter wants her father to die with.

In my case, the guilt that came with the idea of Dad going to his grave knowing his daughter was a hooker was nothing compared to the guilt that came with the fire that killed him being my fault. Do not get me wrong, I did not start it. But if I had done what it took to get the job done properly—as he bet me that I could—the person who did start that fire would have been caught long before now. As part of the Miami Arson Investigation task force, I worked on the streets with the male arson investigators dressed as homeless bums sitting on the street corners with the other degenerates while Mercedes and I posed as street hookers. We had the arsonists on our radar with a bird's-eye view of their strike zones, merchants who hired them to destroy their property to collect insurance or to hide evidence of criminal acts. Miami was under siege in the 1980s with drug manufacturing shops inside old factories, deserted commercial properties, and condemned residential occupancies.

I wondered when a parent's level of support becomes blinded by love, giving the child a false sense of indestructibility emanating as a detriment to society? The answer is this: when a child's level of adoration for their parent is equal to the parent's level of adoration for the child, despite the child being mature enough to see that mutual admiration doesn't allow for the conflict needed to stop the madness and save or nurture a life other than your own

# CHAPTER 2

Denzil Hamilton helped bring me into the sweltering world of Miami in 1951, and in 1958, he saved me from a hellish paralytic life. The least I could have done was to honor his heroism and not let him die with visions of his oldest daughter as a hooker. Some nations burn the dead to free the soul, but no one should burn to death, especially not someone who dedicated his life for others to live in freedom. Dad was a Miami firefighter, and when he was promoted, we called him "Captain Community." A Pikeville, Kentucky football star with a full scholarship to the University of Kentucky, Dad loved the sport. Unfortunately, his college football career came to a halt during his second year when he was drafted into the US Army and stationed in Germany at the height of World War II. During the war years, the American military saw a rapid expansion of its military bases to accommodate the skyrocketing number of young men enlisting and being conscripted. Many of these included former collegiate stars of the football gridiron. Dad was chosen to play halfback on the Army football team. I have photos of his team and of him on a Harley with various German and French ladies. He spoke many times of that team, and just once he divulged the night, they crept along the ground from their foxholes to liberate a concentration camp. I will tell you this: the WWII soldiers did not like to talk about the war when they got home. I had to bug him to get information. He told me about a few skirmishes but quickly reverted back to his days playing football.

Looking back, Miami in 1958 was like any American town in the 1950s: white as sand covering our beaches, just like me. We lived in a modest neighborhood of bungalows built with cinder blocks and each having about a dozen coats of paint. The colors ranged from white, to off-white, to eggshell. When the Miami sun hit them just right, I used to tease my little sister, Sheila, that we were sending signals to aliens.

Mom's aluminum suntan contraption she held under her chin helped add to the illusion and send Sheila's fertile imagination into a tailspin.

Houses went up slowly in the 1950s, and some sat empty for a while, and other lots were just sandy patches we could run around in and perform cartwheels. It was far from the Florida of today where every home has a pool, regardless of its worth. Our yards did not have sprinkler-fed sod. If they turned green it was nature's plan. The "stickers," which were actually sandspurs, were huge. If they were young and green, they did not hurt. But look out for the large, rigid brown spurs that punctured and settled even in callused feet. Kids of the tropics ran barefoot across rocks and hot sand all year round, yet that armor was no defense for a "sticker"! The house next door had a steel swing set that I loved to use. It was not cemented into the ground, so my goal every time I got on was to see how long it took for the support beams to pop in and out of the ground. I would be going so high when it happened that it was like being hypnotized by a pendulum. Up and down, in and out. The family that lived there moved when I was six, so I sort of took ownership of the swing, and Dad mowed the lawn so that was a sign that we had carte blanche approval.

In my short eight years, I believed my parents and neighbors were an exotic and culturally rich group. Of course, not knowing what those words really meant, it is safe to say, I was fascinated by their pasts and the way they told their stories. Down the street was the wise old owl of the neighborhood, Mrs. Achterkirch. To understand her suspicion and worldly advice, all you really needed to know was that she was a German Holocaust survivor; she had the tattooed number on her forearm to prove it. I always wondered how she found her way to our little slice of the world, but I was too afraid to ask because I knew she would tell me. An uncensored old woman of Jewish and German ancestry made for horrifying, sharp-toned tales that never ended soon enough. I am blessed to have known Mrs. Achterkirch and to hear personal experiences of discrimination culminating in torture and so many deaths. It was recognition that brainwashing propaganda and the power of hatred for one specific religion fueled the evils of WWII. Even when the war was over, home-spun sagas permeated innocent minds.

Mom, being from New York City, had an outspoken flair for what she deemed to be good taste. This was com-pounded by the fact that she thought she was psychic. She did not have a neon tarot card sign in the window or anything, but she absolutely trusted her gut, and she did not give anyone else a reason to doubt it either. In fact, her mom, my grandma, also claimed to have the gift, and from what I recall they did make some sort of business of it in New York then drifted South to Cassadaga, Florida, where they bought a cottage and continued their spiritual readings.

Dad, on the other hand, was a Kentucky farm boy the third child and first male of 7 children. His father was a Fuller Brush man and died in a fiery car crash coming around the mountain. After his father's death the whole family was adopted by the church, and all eight of them lived in the back of the sanctuary. He told me many times of having to sleep three boys in one bed and his mom and four girls in the other. They were given steel pails of milk and cornbread all squished into one lumpy mess. He and his siblings loved that concoction and ate it for the rest of their days, and in Miami that was quite appalling. They offered it to me, and I could not even think of tasting it.

He swept Mom off her feet and promised her paradise in Miami, a place where celebrities and presidents vaca-tioned and where he could get a sweet deal on brand new home. He and Mom were the hip version of *Green Acres* before the show even existed.

So, life in Miami when I was born was in many ways the postcard version of the white-picket-fenced American dream. It was a place where bare-bottomed Coppertone kids could frolic in the sand with their puppies, fearless of long-term damage to their skin. In fact, America was so caught up in being free and progressive that it seemed no one was concerned about long-term consequences to their health or the health of their children.

# CHAPTER 3

Children from first to fifth grade lined the halls of our little elementary school, waiting in line for a miracle syrup that a famous doctor, Jonas Salk, invented to prevent the polio disease. It was built up so much that we felt like we were waiting in line for a visit from Santa. The schools had sent home a flyer with his picture. Mom did not like the looks of him.

"Why did he have to go to Russia to test this miracle vaccine?" she asked.

Dad picked up the flyer and read. "It says here he's studied the effects of the new polio vaccine in one hundred adults, and his own wife and children."

In the first eight months of 1957 the Public Health Service reported, out of a total of 3,212 polio cases, there were 1,055 cases of paralysis, or 33.5% of the total. From January 1st to August 1958 there was a total of 1,638 cases of polio, with 801 of them paralytic, or 49% of the total.

On March 26, 1953, American medical researcher Dr. Jonas Salk announces on a national radio show that he has successfully tested a vaccine against poliomyelitis, the virus that causes the crippling polio disease. In 1952—an epidemic year for polio—there were fifty-eight thousand new cases reported in the United States, and more than three thousand died from the disease. For promising eventually to eradicate the disease, which is known as "infant paralysis" because it mainly affects children, Dr. Salk was celebrated as the great doctor-benefactor of his time.

That syrup tasted like grasshopper tar. They claimed it was cherry and dyed it red, but it was more of a reddish brown, like motor oil with red food coloring. As soon as it hit my tongue my gag reflex kicked in, and our school nurse shoved it down my throat. I think she gave me more in fear that I "lost" some the first try. I did not complain, but I do remember spending an extra-long turn at the water fountain. By the time school let out, I had forgotten about it. My bike had a way of making everything right. I think that was the greatest thing about being an American kid in the 1950s, 1960s, and maybe even the 1970s; learning to ride a bike was the equivalent of a driver's license back then. Forget helmets, locks, and boundaries, if you could make those pedals go, no parent worried they would take you too far. I loved to close my eyes and feel the sun and wind on my face and just coast. I felt like a kite, at the mercy of the wind but in charge of my course. I asked Mrs. Achterkirch once if they had bikes in Germany.

"Da," she said. "America didn't invent the bicycle, a German did. But Americans made it a toy." She added this dig like America had ruined the sanctity of hopping on pieces of aluminum with wheels and making them go. "That's kind of neat," I said. "This was invented in Germany and I get to enjoy it in Miami." I hopped off my bike and hugged her. She did not return it, but that was because she did not hug—ever. *Black Beauty* was one of the first books I read and enjoyed. In the back of my mind, I had a goal to break in Mrs. Achterkirch with hugs.

She grabbed me by the shoulders and in her scariest whisper told me, "Planes have started landing in Miami, soon Hell will break loose."

I soon would learn that she was talking about the passenger jets that had just started coming to Miami, it would not be until many years later that I would realize just how prophetic her panicked whisper was.

My bicycle freedom meant that I did not have to have a chaperone as I flew through the neighborhood, but in reality, I had nowhere to go. So, every day after school I would coast to the neighbor's yard and swing—a sort of grounded continuance of my love for soaring in the wind and sun. My little sister Sheila had not gotten her childhood wings yet, so pushing her gently was a way to give her the experience of feeling the wind while maintaining my freedom.

That day, I got an extra serving of reddish-brown grasshopper tar. It was no different—at first. I put my bike on the ground and hopped on the seat, pumping my legs with all of my might until there it was, the in and out of the swing-set legs in the sandy dirt—my signal to let the sun hit my face and coast, hypnotized—*in, out, in, out.*

The front right leg always started first, and when the front left began to lift, I knew it was time to slow. If I let them both go together, the entire swing set would flip backward. I thought it did. I saw the right leg going in and out, and next thing I knew my head was lurching back, then forward. I knew my body was doing something that I had no control over, and I could not do anything but let it go.

My little sister Sheila was a model angel, almost two years younger than me; she was adorable from the moment we met. Her blonde hair cascaded in curls, while mine hung limp in the humidity. I liked being a big sister; it made me feel in control. And Sheila made it easy and fun. Except for the day she found me on the neighbor's swing set circling the drain of death.

"Push me," Sheila said. She hopped on the swing next to me not realizing I could not move. I could not lift my head to look her in the eyes, and even if I could, I do not think my eyes were in their proper place.

"I'm dying."

Sheila squealed like only a five-year-old girl could. She rode her bike home like Margaret Hamilton (another scary Hamilton), who played the wicked witch from the Wizard of Oz yelling, "Daddy! Veronica is dead!"

# CHAPTER 4

I do not remember much about that afternoon, but I swear when the wind blows just right, I can still hear Sheila's screams for help.

I barely remember muttering, "they did this."

My sweet angel must have had nightmares for years. She screamed the entire time she ran, the fastest she ever had.

Dad was home, two doors away, working in the yard with the radio propped up in the window with the news full volume. Mom had a music station and Dad had a news station: that radio dial was like a combination lock clicking between the two on a daily basis.

"Daddy! Veronica is dead! Aliens got her!" Sheila screamed over the lawnmower.

Dad raced to the swing set and pried off my sweaty legs curled under the plastic seat. He picked me up and ran to our tail-finned sedan.

"I can't move my legs. Why can't I move my legs? Am I dead?"

Sheila screamed so loud, siren engineers across the country took note.

"Sheila, sweetie, it's okay, Veronica is going to be okay. Ride and get your mom, tell her to bring her purse."

Dad set me in the back seat.

"I'm sorry," I said through a gush of tears.

Dad hugged me and cupped his big sweaty hands to my nose. He intertwined his fingers like a bird. "This may be the last one I get." He took his thumb that was meant to be my nose and made it morph into a butterfly. He looked out across the yard and pointed. "Look, there it goes, I think it's the prettiest one yet."

In no time, the tail-finned sedan flew me to the hospital emergency room where I was stabilized and diagnosed with polio. The very disease I ate bloody grasshopper tar to avoid getting.

The next day, Mom had me in our family doctor's office ready to decapitate the doctor who tested his vaccine on the Russkies and Miami second graders, Albert Sabin. There was no fire like the one that Dorothy Hamilton could light under a Southerner's ass. Mom's New York fire smoldered until it needed to be stamped out wherever she was. She blew smoke at Dr. Cooper, our family's general practitioner. Mom was not going to let up until she had some answers. She was in Dr. Cooper's office. Mom had these ivory cigarette holders that she wielded like swords to make her point, or to cover the fact that she was just as terrified as I was about what was really going on.

"How is it that the vaccine gave her the very disease it was designed to prevent?" Mom asked.

"All inoculations—"

"You want to see groundbreaking? I'll dig Dr. Jonas Salk's grave."

Mom did not want a scientific rant. She wanted to be heard loud and clear. She wanted everyone within earshot to understand that Dorothy Hamilton from New York City was on the case.

I remember her cigarette smoke streaming from her nose like a bull as she had her say. The ash was as long as the ivory holder. Even if I grow ancient with Alzheimer's, the entire surreal incident of "the polio invasion," as it came to be known, will forever be etched in my memory. Like a dinosaur fossil, I was an anomaly. Out of all the children in my school and in Florida who lined up for that grasshopper tar, I was the only one who got polio: one in a million.

Dr. Cooper measured his response as he put an ashtray in front of Mom. She stamped out her cigarette, and hot embers flew in their faces. Dr. Cooper stepped into the hallway, for fresh air I thought, but he returned with a small wheelchair. Mom shut up as the reality set in. He wheeled it next to the table I sat on and carefully slid me into it.

"The good news is, it's a nonparalytic form of polio. Her symptoms should gradually clear up. In fact, I bet she's dancing on the beach by the New Year."

He showed Mom the controls of the chair, which she insisted was not necessary. As she pushed me out, he held the door open for us.

"You better hope she is," she said.

Dr. Cooper gave her a curious look.

"Dancing. You better hope she becomes a world class dancer."

By then, I was embarrassed.

At home Mom told Dad all about it as he inspected the wheelchair. He shook his head at her as she recalled how she put the doctor in his place.

"Doc Coop didn't give her the vaccine. He's not to blame."

"Well why not? Why do not doctors give their patients vaccines? Letting the school do it is like letting her five-year-old sister Sheila style my hair."

"Hey!" Sheila chimed in, "Can I?" Little did Mom know that Sheila would excel at the Barbizon, the international modeling and acting school, and would be walking runways all over the world.

Dad laughed and spun the chair up on its big wheels. "This will have to be your new ride for a bit, think you're up to it? Ah, of course you are, you can handle anything life throws you, isn't that right, Roni?

What could I do, but nod?

I learned to manage the wheelchair just fine, and in some ways, it was better than my bike, except that I had to be driven to and from school. After the first few weeks, I began to use crutches and the wheelchair, and then Mom enrolled me in ballet class to get my balance and strength back. The thing is, I was uncoordinated before the polio, and no amount of ballet was going to change that. One thing was different after the polio, however: I became pigeon-toed. I did not think much of it and just figured my feet would straighten the stronger my legs got. One day I heard Mom talking to the ballet instructor about it, so I knew she noticed. No one ever spoke of it—especially when it looked like it was not getting any better.

Sheila, on the other hand, was pretty much born a ballerina and her copying my practice looked better than most of the students in the class.

Luckily for Dr. Cooper, he was right, and the symptoms began to fade more each day, so he did not have to face the wrath of Dorothy Hamilton.

Mom and Dad loved to host parties at our house. It was a small bungalow, so if a dozen people showed up it felt like standing room only. On New Year's Eve they had about thirty people over. A few brought their own kids, and we all raided Mom's kitchen cabinets to bang pots and pans at midnight. We were so loud that Mrs. Achterkirch went home. She could not handle loud noises—another shocking side effect from WWII.

Sheila and I were passed out in the living room while Mom and Dad cleaned up, so I did not consciously hear the news break in over the radio. Fidel Castro and his revolution had overtaken Cuba, forcing Batista to flee the country. Dad loved the news, so I tried to keep up with it. But even if I had been awake to hear about Castro's takeover, I could not have known that my world was about to change forever.

# CHAPTER 5

The hardest thing about the wheelchair and leg braces was not being able to go to the beach. We lived in Miami after all, so being banned from the beach was like being banned from the backyard. So, I was more excited for New Year's Day than I was Christmas. Ever since Dr. Cooper mentioned that I should be dancing on the beach by New Year's, it was etched in my mind that we would all go to the beach that day. And since my physical therapy seemed to be working, there really was no reason not to stick to his word—except for the fact that my parents had been up partying all night.

We made it to the beach around lunchtime. As Mom "people watched" from the blanket, Dad forced an umbrella to stand upright in the sand, and Sheila and I ran to the surf. Sheila started twirling like a ballerina. I did a half pirouette and then let a wave knock me down. I could see Mom grab Dad's arm to stop what he was doing to see if I needed help. I got up quickly and danced with Sheila so they would not do something horrible, like make me sit out.

While Sheila and I goofed off, I glanced back and saw Dad say something to Mom with a smile, and then he began stringing up our kite. I could tell he had faith in my strength. A few minutes later he ran to us like a big kid with the kite soaring overhead.

Bear in mind that this was the late 1950s, and kites were basic, nothing like the elaborate works of art that fly over South Beach today. But Dad had painted flames and big cartoon eyes on our white diamond. So, to us this was more than a work of art—it was like a family mascot.

"Firefly!" we squealed, as Dad steered it to dive over the water.

Then a low roar drowned out the sound of the waves and grew more deafening by the second. We ran out of the surf and grabbed on to Dad's legs.

"Should we duck and cover?" I asked.

Just then Sheila screamed, "Firefly!"

Dad realized what had happened before she screamed. The string broke. We all turned to see the family mascot hover in an air pocket and then dive into the sea. We did not have much time to be devastated because just then a pair of Pan Am 707 jet planes flew overhead; they were so low, I thought they snapped the kite string. Sheila and I did not even ask; we just got into duck-and-cover position by instinct since Fairlawn Elementary instituted bomb drills in all classrooms. My job was to take down the flag that was mounted high on the wall inside our classroom. I practiced stepping on a desk to reach it. I think that responsibility forecasted my future.

Passenger jets were still new to our world, and I am guessing the pilots did not have the proper air space regulations quite ironed out. When I lifted my head, I could not help but see that Dad was in awe of the giant silver birds. By then, Mom had joined us and was singing Frank Sinatra's hit, *"Come fly with me."*

"That, my girls, is the new face of freedom," Dad said. Little did he know that inside the planes, Cubans thanked God to be alive.

"If you can afford it," Mom piped in with her NYC sarcasm. "How much you want to bet Frank Sinatra is on one of those planes?"

"Who cares who's on them, let's eat!" Dad managed to tickle us all at the same time as we scurried back to the blanket.

Before we left the beach, I ran back across the sand and saluted the surf. "You served us well, Firefly, rest in pieces." I thought that was the saying until that day. Mom and Dad set me straight once they stopped laughing their heads off.

# CHAPTER 6

Not long after that, Dad was in the garage giving my bike a tune up. He had pulled it out from behind the Christmas decorations in the corner and slid the wheelchair in its place. I had been waiting for this moment almost as much as I had waited for New Year's Day.

"It's fine, it hasn't been that long." I said hoping to speed up the master tinker.

"We can't have you go and get hurt in a wreck because of bad tires and rusty alignment," he said. "If you're not going to be safe for you, be safe for me, and besides, I'm done."

He flipped over my bike, and I yanked it from him before he could wipe it down. I will never forget that bike and its lilac frame with a white seat and a white plastic basket that had matching lilac flowers on it—plastic of course.

I hopped on and tore down the driveway. But my run was cut short as quickly as it started. I skidded to a stop, and Dad hurried out.

"Take it easy, you forgot the power of mobility," he said.
"I did not."

No sooner had the words come out of my mouth, and
Dad saw it, too. A station wagon, so loaded that it sagged,
rolled past our driveway. It followed a slick tail-finned
sedan. There was more. Behind the station wagon were
three more cars all similarly overloaded. The cars had the
windows down, and we could see the faces of the passen-
gers. Not one of them smiled, even though they seemed
to be in some sort of parade. All of them had jet-black
hair, except for a handful of elders who had turned gray,
and their skin was tan, so they did not need aluminum
shields when they lay out in the sun.

Mom and Sheila joined us in the driveway; none of us
uttered a word. I could see Mrs. Achterkirch on her step,
and the neighbor across the street was peeking out of her
blinds. The tail-finned sedan stopped, and a man got out.

"He's fancy," Sheila said. Mom pulled her close so she
would not run to the cars, I guess.

The man pointed the cars in his caravan to the empty
houses on the block, and as they followed his direction,
the residents all came out to see who was moving in.

"Stay put," Dad told us.

"There he goes, Captain Community," Mom said.

Our eyes were glued on every car as they emptied, like
there was a drive-in movie screen at each empty house
they stopped at. Men, women, children, and grandpar-
ents piled out and tried to figure out where they were.
To me, they looked like royalty. They were all dressed in
their Sunday best, and I knew it was Saturday because

Dad had promised I could ride my bike on Saturday. The women wore dresses of colorful linen, and they had on red lipstick that was brighter than clowns' noses at the circus. Even the old ladies of the bunch had circus-clown red lips. I swear I could smell their perfume, but Mom would not hear of it. The men and boys were in pressed pleated slacks with tucked- in collared shirts and freshly shined shoes. Their tanned faces shone as much as their heads of black hair. They must have been sweating to death cooped up in those cars with that perfume. The girls were the most surprising. Breathtaking, really. Most of them were wearing white linen dresses with shiny white shoes to match. Everything about them sparkled, even their bobby pins.

"Princesses," Sheila said.

"They certainly don't shop at Montgomery Ward," Mom answered.

"I wonder if they were on those planes we saw at the beach?" I said. "They certainly look rich enough to fly."

Sheila startled at the thought. "Aliens," she announced.

I had grown so used to teasing Sheila about aliens that there was no way I was going to try and convince her otherwise. I bit my lips together in tight affirmation and nodded. Mom elbowed me. "Ow."

Dad turned and shot us a glare that meant "shut up" just as he was about to talk to the man who led the royal alien caravan.

Mrs. Achterkirch tried to nose her way into Dad's introduction, but he turned his shoulder just enough as she approached that she got the hint. She came and stood by us instead.

"I wonder if they paid cash?" Mom said.

Mrs. Achterkirch laughed aloud, making Sheila jump. "*Flee-ers*," she said. "Lucky Batistianos flee to paradise, perfectly legal, they have it all handed to them." She rubbed the numbers on her wrist with her knobby thumb. She rubbed it so much, Mom caught me watching and shot me a look like I should not.

"With fleas come exterminators," Mrs. Achterkirch added.

Like a lot of things about her, that line about fleas and exterminators stuck in my head. It practically echoed there when she said it then. And even now, it occasionally surfaces in my memory, and I am somehow reminded that all change includes both good and bad. I had studied Mrs. Achterkirch long enough to know that when she rubbed the numbers tattooed on her wrist, she was upset. At the time, I had no idea what they stood for, but as I grew into the changing landscape of Miami, those numbers on her skin and our new neighbors became pieces to my lifelong puzzle of how America can be the strongest but also the most vulnerable country in the world.

# CHAPTER 7

My life outside of school suddenly became much more educational than life in school. I had always loved listening to the news with Dad, not because I knew what they were talking about, but because it was like I could see his brain working as he agreed or disagreed with what was being reported. More often than not it gave me an *in* to the adult conversations at the dinner table. That night, I learned that the families that invaded our neighborhood were not fleas, royalty, or even aliens: they were Cubans. They were forced out of Cuba when this skinny guy with a beard barged in and took over their country. They came to America legally to be safe from this madman, and Miami was closest to home, so they were allowed to move here. Or at least that is what the man in the sharp suit explained to Dad when he was playing Captain Community. Mom was not so sure.

"They are mob-funded, I bet you, sure as the sun will shine tomorrow. They own casinos and drug cartels, and they want to make Miami their new home. I know I saw at least one of those families brought a maid," she rambled on to Dad.

"They have made Miami their home, at least until they can get their leader restored in Cuba."

"I'm just sayin' it's not going to happen."

Interesting or not, there is only so much news a nine-year-old can take before falling asleep. Sheila and I drooled on the floor in front of the TV that night, while Mom and Dad learned about Fidel Castro. Dad always teased Mom that she was more accurate than the news, but with houses full of upset Cubans, Mom's radar was apparently on overload, and trying to grasp it all in one night was giving her a headache.

"What's the verdict?" Dad asked.

"I'm tired," she answered.

"Get some rest, everyone's knack gets out of whack once in a while."

"Knack, *smack*. I don't have to have government clearance to know that this is a can of worms."

She picked up Sheila for bed and told Dad to turn off the television. "Poor girls are going to have nightmares about aliens in camouflage," she said and turned off the TV herself and tapped me to get up for bed.

All I remember was that Dad came over and kissed us goodnight and then turned the TV back on. "I would think you of all would understand the need to know everything about where your neighbors come from." He was mad because when you turned a television on in those days you had to wait for the picture tubes to warm up. Rumor had it that if you went from off to on too quickly, the tubes would burst. I never touched the on/off for that reason, besides the fact that I was not allowed to. Televisions were still revered as a luxury in the late 1950s. Even though by then most homes had them, TVs certainly were not in multiple rooms or something that children monopolized. In our house, the TV was as much a staple as the family car. And so, its maintenance fell to Dad.

# CHAPTER 8

Mrs. Achterkirch's husband worked as TV repairman. Upon arriving from Germany, he had to choose a profession. Jewish people locked up in concentration camps in Germany had minimal food and water for survival, so when arriving in the United States, TVs were weird boxes with pictures and sound. Divine intervention led Mr. Achterkirch to a TV on the fritz. After fooling around with it for an hour, to his surprise, he had fixed it.

Magically he became a self-proclaimed expert TV repairman. He had no professional connections in Miami, so he traveled into the Everglades to a town called Immokalee. Two Thousand years ago, the region was occupied by Calusa Indians. Centuries later it was populated by the Seminole and Miccosukee Indians. The swamps were drained in the region, and agriculture became the dominant industry.

In 1872, European-American hunters, trappers, Indian traders, cowmen, and missionaries moved to Immokalee. Mr. Achterkirch was aware of the town. His German ancestors from were among the settlers. It was put on the map when the Atlantic Coast Line Railroad was extended from Haines City south of the town.

As he muttered that Mom was going to burn out the tubes, I groggily stood up to follow Mom out. "Can aliens grow beards?" I asked.

"No, honey, they're bald," Mom said.

After a good night's sleep, I was ready to go soar on my bike and scope out the new neighborhood residents. It was Sunday morning, so things were quiet. Dad finished reading his paper, and Mom was cleaning up the remains of breakfast when I announced I was going to ride my bike.

"I'll go out with you, see if any of our new neighbors needs a hand," Dad said.

"Well maybe I'll see if any of them need to go to the salon," Mom joked.

I hopped on my bike as Dad looked up and down the street. "What do I do if the kids are out?" I asked.

"Offer to be a friend but mind your business," Dad said. By then I was already down the block. "And your balance!" he added.

I pedaled my pigeon-toes as fast and hard as I could, no doubt trying to cram three months of no bike power into one hour. I zipped around our block, never letting up. I watched my knees go around and round, the dots on the faded asphalt blurring underneath. I laughed to myself, and next thing I knew I was rounding the corner near my house again, and I finally let up. Coasting down our peaceful road, the sun blazed in my face. I closed my eyes and let it soak in. Putting all of my strength and faith into my legs, I raised my arms as if to fly—it gave me the confidence to know everything was back to normal in my life, even if only for a second.

"*Aye, Dios Mio*," the old woman said.

I opened my eyes, and the true reality of my life came crashing back. One of the Cuban grandmothers stood in the middle of our street, lost, and crossing herself in prayer, sure she was about to die. I pumped my brakes and jingled my dime store bike bell.

"No hablo Ingles," the old woman screamed, even though I did not say anything.

I swerved my bike to avoid her and jumped off so I would not fall on my newly functioning legs. At the same time Mrs. Achterkirch ran from her yard and pulled the old woman away. I ran to them both as the front wheel of my upended bike whirled in the dead air.

"I am so sorry," I said.

Mrs. Achterkirch translated and continued speaking to the old woman in Spanish. Mrs. Achterkirch spoke seven languages; she told me that once you knew one, the rest were easy—if that one was not English. English, she said was a language that had too many cooks but no master chef.

We were all surprised to see a young Cuban girl wheel my bike to us. Lourdes Cartaya was my age but well beyond my years. She stood there in a white dress with colorful flowers embroidered around her chest. She may have been nine, but I could not help and notice that she was ready for a training bra as she gently wheeled the bike to me. The old woman exploded in a tearful confession. Her Spanish was so fast that I was thankful I spoke English—nice and slow.

Mrs. Achterkirch translated what the old woman said. "She says she was almost killed, and she wants to go home. Her granddaughter is telling her that her home is here."

Sure enough, the girl named Lourdes was pointing to the house they had just moved into. I felt sorry for the old woman; you could tell she was scared and that she felt she did not belong. For the first time I realized how nearly every house on our street looked the same. Sure, some had different-colored shutters or an extra flowerpot on the step or wreath on the door, but I had to admit that if I had just been uprooted from the only home I'd ever known and dropped into this neighborhood, I'd have a hard time finding my way.

As Spanish continued to zip back and forth between them, the old woman finally tottered back to the house they had just moved into. The houses that the federal government provided to the refugees had been abandoned for a few years, so now the government owned them. The yard was fried from sun and the lack of water. Weeds surrounded some native elephant ears thriving under a big old avocado tree. In that moment I remember wishing we had a tree like that, and then I realized that they moved into the house with my swing! *I must make friends with this family*, I thought.

We watched as the old woman went inside as if we all wanted to make sure she would get that far.

Lourdes turned to me and in broken English said, "Sawy"

I did not know how much English she spoke, so instead of trying to talk about it, I just offered her my bike. "You can try it," I said. "I'll wait if you want to go change your dress."

Instead, Lourdes climbed on in her dress. I liked that. I did not know how to deal with a princess, and this showed me that deep down, she was just like me. Mrs. Achterkirch and I watched her get the bike going and peddle toward my house.

"Mi Española is a little rusty, but I'm fairly sure the old one said something like 'take me to your leader.'"

It was like Mrs. Achterkirch timed her innuendo so that the sun would provide the most dramatic emphasis. The way it beamed on her face outlined her already sharp features with even sharper shadows. I knew she was trying to freak me out.

"Save it for Sheila," I said and ran to catch up to Lourdes.

# CHAPTER 9

Lourdes and I hung out for the rest of the day. She spoke good English, and we quickly worked through a way to deal with things about each other that we could not understand. She was amazed to see Dad at all of the new arrivals' houses helping cut the lawn and making sure everyone had what they needed. Dad was thrilled to see that I had befriended one of the newcomers. But in all honesty, I was thrilled to have a friend my age and an exotic one at that. Lourdes from Cuba became my first best friend the same day I almost ran over her grandma with my bike.

Mom and Dad organized a block party to welcome everyone, or rather Dad wanted to welcome everyone, and Mom wanted to "get to know" them, which was another way of saying she was going to use her prophetic gift to gather gossip.

Dad manned the grill in our backyard, while Sheila, Lourdes, and I led the children's' entertainment with bubbles and beach balls. Lourdes helped communicate to the other Cuban children. There was one Cuban boy named Mario who was ten but acted like he was a teenager: he thought he was cool, which only made him look like a fool. Lourdes and I ran past him with Sheila on our heels. At first, he sneered at us like he could not be bothered, so we just kept on going. Lourdes warned me not to take his bait. But soon after we passed, he started screaming like I thought only Sheila could. We turned around to see him freaking out over a lizard that had dropped onto his shoulder.

Lizards are like flies in Florida. They come in all shapes and sizes and scurry about just as much as people do. Most importantly, though, they are completely harmless if you can overlook their poop. Back then they were our best source of pest control. The art of catching lizards is a rite of passage for Floridian children, but I guess well-to-do people from Cuba had maids for things like that.

Sheila and I had fun dressing up and latching lizards to our ears as jewelry. We squeezed them gently, placed them near our earlobes, and they opened their mouths and took a bite. The bite did not hurt our earlobes, but when a lizard latched on to toes it *really* hurt.

# CHAPTER 10

I walked back to Mario and picked the lizard up off his collar, freeing it in the bushes. Lourdes nicknamed me "the lizard tamer." Mario tried to save face by claiming it was biting him. Meanwhile everyone was laughing and pretty much ignoring him—he hated to be ignored. Lourdes's father had just turned on some Cuban music, while Dad had just delivered the first plate of charred burger. When there is good food, a lively crowd, and music that makes even old people want to wiggle, what is not to laugh about? Sure, it had only been a couple of days, but so far, our new neighborhood seemed like it had changed for the better.

As the reality of the workweek came around, I was excited to be able to ride my bike to and from school once again. But on the way home I saw all of the Cuban kids hanging out, hot and bored. I stopped to talk to Lourdes.

"How come you don't have school?" I asked.

"We did in Cuba. I liked it," she said.

I wondered if they would get enrolled in my school or if they were just on a long vacation until they went back home.

"I usually have a peanut butter sandwich and watch TV after school, do you want to come over?"

I introduced Lourdes to *I Love Lucy*. It actually helped her learn some more English because it was the episode where they went to Mexico and Lucy became a bullfighter. We all had a good laugh.

That night at dinner I asked Dad if the Cuban kids would have to go to school. He thought it was a good question, but before he could answer, he got a phone call, and Mom shooed Sheila and me out of the kitchen. Mom stayed and pretended to wash dishes, but all of us knew she was listening to the call.

Dad was captain of his fire station's 14-C shift, so it was not much of a stretch to call him Captain Community. He was always being asked to coordinate something, and he did not mind, because back then Miami was so sleepy that they had a lot of free time at the station. When he hung up the phone, Sheila and I hid behind the open bi-fold door that separated the kitchen from the living room.

"I have to collect all the men and take them for a meeting," Dad said.

Mom came over and closed the bi-fold door. I know that she knew we could still hear it was not exactly an air-tight seal. But that's how Mom rolled; she liked to constantly remind us of the fact that nothing got by her. She used to part the back of her hair to show us the eyes she warned about, but she quickly pushed her hair back nonchalantly, so we never saw them.

"What are they doing, gathering a hunt? You're busy enough."

"No. Just the Cuban men, they want to train them... to fight their own battle."

"Homework better be done, and teeth brushed by the time these dishes are done," Mom shouted. That was our notice that it was not okay to listen anymore.

Dad went out and knocked on our new neighbors' doors, explaining that the men needed to go to this meeting in the morning. When he was leaving that morning, I was off to school, and I asked him if he could talk to them about school for the kids because they were bored out of their minds. This soon became my first lesson in life: "Be careful what you wish for."

# CHAPTER 11

By the time I got out of school, the meeting had left chaos on the home front. All the Cuban men over the age of eighteen were being sent off to Homestead, a town outside of Miami of farm fields and a military base. Their already confused and homesick families were in the streets crying and blessing themselves like they would never see their men again. I zipped my bike down the street, and all I could hear were Spanish wails and pleas for them to call. I saw Lourdes with her grandma and mother; all of them had swollen eyes from crying.

I walked my bike up the driveway where Mom and Mrs. Achterkirch were standing with Sheila. Dad was helping the men get into vehicles.

"You should go get your friend," Mrs. Achterkirch said.

"What do I say?"

"Ask her to come over, we'll find something to keep you entertained while this plays out," Mom said.

I really did not want to cross through the mayhem, and I felt a tremendous pressure to figure out something amazing to say. I had it in my mind that I was going to ask her how to say "Thank you for being a friend" in Spanish, but I was going to do it word by word to surprise her. As I made it across the street, I saw Mario on the roof of their house. His Dad was leaving but also trying to get him to come down and say goodbye. Mario threw a rock at him.

I was horrified and by the time I got to Lourdes, I forgot my plan and just hugged her instead. Lourdes's mom was hugging her dad, which gave me the idea. Her grandma was standing there with a bag packed, ready to go with the men.

"Cuba libre!" she shouted with her wrinkled fist in the air.

Lourdes pulled her grandma away and spoke to her in Spanish, trying to explain that she could not go with them.

I went inside Lourdes's house with her and her grandma and Lourdes explained, "It's called the Cuba project. The American government wants to train the men of Cuba to fight to get our country back."

"How long will they be gone?"

"As long as it takes."

I had made a promise to Lourdes that she could meet me at my house after school the next day, and we'd hang out to get her away from the drama and worry of her mom and grandma. So I pedaled harder than I ever had, even before the polio incident, and when I got home, Lourdes was there in the front yard—with dozens of other Cuban kids of all ages, some I hadn't even met yet. I was sure that she understood me and that I had not told her to invite everyone. Still, all I could think about was how to explain this to Mom. Then I saw Dad, and I knew it was not a misunderstanding: *this was more news.*

# CHAPTER 12

I got off my bike and walked it toward Dad, where he took it and carefully chose his words.

"You know how you asked about their schooling? Well, how would you like to walk them all to school?"

"Sure, I can show them where it is."

"Not just once, every day. I need your help in making sure they understand where to go, how to sign in so they can understand on their own."

"I have to walk them every day, both ways?" I could feel Dad pulling my bike farther away. I had just gotten it back, and now the one moment of peace, of freedom, I enjoyed, was about to be taken from me again. "It's not fair." I turned in my huff and saw a sea of big brown eyes staring at me, including Lourdes's.

"Careful wishing," Dad said. "It's the right thing to do." He kissed my head, and my fate was sealed.

Just then, two boxy wood-paneled trucks pulled up on our block, and Dad went to greet them. It took me a minute to realize they were delivering food supplies. I was still in shock with my new responsibility, and Dad was off coordinating another effort—all for these people who landed on our doorstep unannounced less than a week earlier. I was sad, confused, and excited all at once, but more than anything I was in awe of my dad. He was Captain Community. He lugged boxes of jars of peanut butter, plantains, and rice. There were no Cuban men to help, and the American men were mostly off at work. I watched Dad sort a little of each into one box and offer it to Mario's mom, and she shook her head in confusion. He told Mario to carry it home for her, and Mario turned and ran off. The supplies kept coming off the truck, and Dad was dripping with sweat sorting it all out. One of the smaller children took a jar of peanut butter, and Dad stopped to open it for him. The tiny child began shoveling the peanut butter into his chubby cheeks with his fingers.

That whole scene is still etched in my memory to this day. I wiped my selfish tears away and ran to help Dad sort and deliver the rations.

Before the last truck closed its back door, the driver handed me a heavy bag of limes. "It will keep the scurvy away from them," he said.

I had no idea what scurvy was but knew enough to believe that if the government defined it as a threat then it must be some Cuban disease. Dad took the limes and tossed a couple into each ration box we had sorted.

"Thanks for your help," he said. "You'll make a fine leader someday."

Just like that, at the age of nine, my first job was with the government: babysitting Cuban refugees. Dad said it would be temporary, but I felt good because he was proud of me, so it did not really matter if it was for a day, week, or life. I had Dad's approval and support.

Once a week, like the ice cream man, those trucks pulled up and I sorted the boxes as they were unloaded. Lourdes and Sheila helped deliver the sorted boxes to the Cuban households. I needed Lourdes to explain and translate; at first the Cuban families did not understand that these trucks were a gift to them from the US government. After a while, they realized there was only so much you could do with peanut butter. The food ration deliveries were the easiest part of my "government job," as Dad called it. Soon, my first lesson in careful wishing became a source of great pride as I sorted and wrangled all of the Cuban children to and from school every single day. Being an embryonic Virgo, I had them lined up by size, so I did not lose sight of the smallest ones. I showed them the best way to lug their books and supplies. This part was bittersweet for me, considering my white plastic bike basket with plastic lilac flowers had been my book bag for the past couple of years. After the first couple of days, we fell into a routine. And like a long line of ducklings we paraded up and down the road, to and from school. It was becoming less painful to see my bike gathering dust in the garage. Between delivering the rations, and making sure everyone understood their homework, my first government job left me little time to soar down the street with my eyes closed, much less think about it.

Every day was another surprise; if Mario wasn't stirring the pot of trouble, or someone's mom wasn't having a meltdown of soap opera proportions because their man was gone, our cultures were constantly testing and redefining what was considered normal.

One day, I went with Lourdes to her house to deliver the week's rations, and we walked in on her grandma with the TV blaring, she was singing the jingle to the Slinky commercial.

"*A Sleenky, a Sleenky*," she sang in severely broken English.

Lourdes and I let out a giggle and a snort and scared the apron right off her, which only made us laugh more.

I dutifully unpacked their box as Lourdes calmed her "Abuela," thinking that the arrival of their box of food would give her something to focus on. I handed her the new jar of peanut butter, and she spit.

I thought maybe somehow, in the way I handed it to her, I had offended some Cuban peanut butter ritual. But then she went to the cabinet and revealed a full shelf of nothing but jars of government-supplied peanut butter. Thinking she made her point, "Abuela," went to the sink to wash her hands of the matter. Reflexively she flipped the switch nearby, and the garbage disposal roared to life. She hurled the jar of peanut butter at "*el monstruo*," and it shattered.

I ran to shut off the disposal before she hurt herself and tried to explain what it was. I pointed to their trash can: "garbage." Then I pointed to the drain: "disposal."

"*Que? Monstruo.*" Then Abuela spit on the broken jar of peanut butter.

Lourdes stayed clear, she was out of her league on this translation and just as concerned as her grandma.

I separated the broken glass from the goopy peanut butter, once the glass was tossed away, I shoved the peanut butter down the drain and turned on the *monstruo*.

They watched the peanut butter get eaten alive and disappear down the drain. After an awfully long few seconds, Grandma jumped up like a little girl and clapped, "Si!"

Lourdes heard *American Bandstand* come on TV and pulled me away from the lesson. As we ran to the living room, I could hear Grandma shoving more peanut butter down the drain and singing commercial jingles.

"See the U.S.A... *en yo Chebrolay.*"

# CHAPTER 13

That night at dinner, I was excited to tell the peanut butter story to my family, but the conversation quickly steered me away from highlighting anything that could be considered ungrateful on the part of our Cuban neighbors.

I twirled my spaghetti, waiting for the right moment for Dad to take a bite and set aside the *Miami Herald*. It never came.

"Kennedy announced he's running," Dad said.

"There's a surprise," Mom shot back.

Dad gave her one of his thousand-word looks.

"Of course, he'll win." She answered without missing a beat, trying to interpret what he was thinking.

Dad may have been Captain Community, but Mom was command central. I do not know if it was because of her innate intuitive skills, or her ability to multitask like a short-order cook in a one-grill town. Even as a child I was amazed at how she orchestrated so many different conversations, tasks, and emotions without breaking a sweat—in Miami no less.

She especially liked to use Sheila's size and innocence to pull Dad's nose out of the news. She poked at her and motioned for her to pop her head up under Dad's paper. The only thing more jarring than a face coming between a man and his evening paper was when it was a pint-sized, spaghetti-faced angel with blonde ringlets.

Mom left it in Sheila's curious mind to come up with the words to say on such occasions.

"If Veronica stops ballet, will her legs stop working again?" Sheila asked Dad.

Dad not only took his nose out of the paper; he put the paper down altogether. I have to say, I was a little startled by the question myself.

"Stand up, Roni," Dad said.

I stood as if for inspection—spine straight, chin out, shoulders back.

"Gams of a racehorse," Dad said.

I was not sure what "gams" were, but they sounded glamorous, and I knew racehorses had good legs. So, I was confident that I passed, until Dad used his big black fireman boot to discretely push my toes to point forward instead of inward. I slinked back to my spaghetti. Dad sat down, tweaked my nose, and made a small butterfly out of his pinkies. I remember blushing. The table was so quiet that I could feel the embarrassment trying to escape through my face.

"I showed Lourdes's grandma what a garbage disposal was today."

"Did she ask you to?" Mom asked. Dad inhaled some noodles and a meatball, half picking his paper up again.

"Soon as they claim their country everything around here will be back the way it was." Sheila clapped, but I was a little lost—what did this have to do with my story? Clearly there was an adult side to this conversation that I was not picking up on. Mom plopped another meatball on Dad's plate.

"Our country is built by guests," he said.

"Who decide to stay," Mom added.

"Unless someone picks a fight, America makes guests feel welcome, it's what we do."

"I saw rust on my bike," I blurted.

"I'll get some royal jelly," Dad told me before getting back to the adult talk. "There's too many of them to stay for good."

# CHAPTER 13

"Thank God, Kennedy is running," Mom said. "How come he can run with the Cubans here, but Veronica can't ride her bike?" Sheila asked. I thought she made a valid point. "He's running for election to run our country," Dad explained. "If he is elected, the Cubans can go home home, and she'll be free to ride, believe you me."

"Believe you me," Sheila repeated.

From that moment on I was a big fan of this Kennedy guy. I carried out my government duties as if they would help John Fitzgerald Kennedy become president. In my mind, if as a government worker I did the best job I could, then the best man would be a shoo-in to lead the country. Florida schools were not the most informative in guidance counseling at the time.

Our school parades began to run like a well-oiled regiment. In fact, I remember telling the kids that lining up and walking like a team was what their dads were learning to do—and this was all it took. After school once a week Sheila helped me sort and deliver the rations. I remember squeezing a lime into a young kid's mouth, and she cried like I was feeding her acid. Sheila had the idea of making limeade, which was brilliant. I would have never thought of it with my ineptitude in the kitchen.

The school was in no way prepared to navigate translating for these kids, so they were not learning anything. When I realized this, I felt like I finally understood Mom when she had to pull out her New York method of purposeful persuasion.

I began holding tutoring sessions after school to help the Cuban children with their schoolwork. It meant that I did not get home till it was nearly dark. I did not mind really, but one night as I walked up the driveway the mosquitoes were particularly annoying. As I beat myself senseless trying to combat them, I noticed my bike. It was tucked against the garage behind a bush, and a giant spider was using the plastic lilac flowers for a bed. I do not know if it was because I was tired, itchy, hungry, or pre-hormonal, but my eyes filled with tears watching that spider enjoying my bike more than I ever had. The mosquitoes pulled me out of it though, as I smacked myself hard enough in the head to snap me back to the reality of smelling Mom's fried chicken.

I was never at the top of my class but teaching kids about my country and language seemed to come naturally, and in many ways, it helped me learn, too. One thing is for sure, I learned how confusing the English language is. There are countless words that sound the same but are spelled differently and mean entirely different things. The first challenge that tipped me off was the word *too*. Not to be confused with *two*, or *to*.

# CHAPTER 14

We had this patch of field in the neighborhood that was perfect for stargazing: in 1960 that was a thing for kids who were itching to get out of the house. One night after their men left, I invited the older Cuban kids, and Dad lit citronella pots for us to help keep the mosquitoes away. Mario came along, but it was only to get away from his house, not because he cared about spending time with any of us. While we sat in the grass waving our tiny smoke sticks and sharing horribly inaccurate facts about the constellations, Mario straddled between a picnic table and tree, poking at lizards with a stick.

"Die, evil monsters," he said.

"You better learn to love them, come next summer, you'll be out here every night just to pray for a breeze," I said.

"Next summer? You're crazy, we'll be home," he said. This time he jabbed and broke off the tip off his stick.

I could still see the look of defeat on his face.

"And now you've gone and angered them, and they won't eat mosquitoes for you," I teased him, and everyone laughed.

"Why do you hate lizards so much?" Sheila asked.

"We had more in Havana than here, they were bigger dos." Mario said.

"You mean too," I said.

"*Si*, that's what I said, *dos*."

"*Dos* is two, not *also*."

I think we saw Mario's mind blow, but I must admit, he covered well. He took his flashlight and lit the underside of his face like he was going to tell us a ghost story. Instead he told us a story about his father's position in Cuba before they had to flee and how it led to his disgust of lizards.

"My Papi was a judge, and in Cuba, judges held a lot of power over everyone, except Santeria, the crooks and murderers. So they pay Santeria spooks to cast spells to set them free and the bad guy's workers who weren't in jail would deliver things like rotten chicken guts and herbs to our door in the middle of the night—nasty stinking things that were supposedly cursed to make my father let them free. One morning, when I was little, I was the first awake and I opened the front door and stepped in a bloody pile of I don't know what." Mario dropped the flashlight, clearly upset by the memory— even though he did his best to be cool.

Sheila was so into the story that she ran over and held the flashlight for him.

"I screamed so loud, I woke not only the whole house, but the whole street," he said. "I thought my foot was bleeding off, it was covered in so much. My parents came running to me, but before they got there a lizard had climbed onto my foot and was licking the blood off my toes. I was in shock, too afraid to move. Ever since, I want to see all lizards die."

I do not know about the others, but I was not sure if he was finished and Mario was so intensely focused on this violent memory, we were all a little too freaked out to interrupt him.

Just then an alligator bellowed. I knew just where it came from.

"Two blocks over, Big Al lives in the canal. He usually does that when he's looking for a girlfriend," I said.

"Does it work?" Lourdes asked.

I cracked up laughing.

"He's an alligator, you want to ask?" Sheila was profoundly serious about the dangers and reality of our nature.

"I meant does he come here, onshore?" Lourdes asked.

"Only if it rains," I said.

Just then, a flash of heat lightning raced across the sky. I could not help but laugh at tough-guy Mario's paranoia.

"Relax, it's not like he's a giant lizard or something," I said.

"Any living thing that can break its tail and grow it new again in order to escape cannot be trusted," Mario said.

The rain came down in spurts, and that was all it took for Mario to hightail it home.

# CHAPTER 15

Rainy season in South Florida lasts most of the year but peaks in the summertime. For some crazy reason, Florida likes it when kids start school in August; it is the hottest part of summer across the country, but in Florida has inferno heat. You have also got hurricane season at its worst from August to October. We don't have snow days, but it's my belief that there's no difference in the six to ten inches of snow that closes schools in cold climates to a day of downpours that equals the same amount of rain in Florida. It is the same inches and the same water; one is just colder than the other. Trust me, when it is your job to hustle dozens of children to and from school, and the sky opens with sheets of rain like guillotines made of black clouds, everyone turns into lost, hysterical ducklings. After a couple of these deluges, I came up with a plan for seeking shelter depending where we were along the way home from school.

As the saying goes when it rains it pours. While I became a momma duck, squawking to keep the neighborhood newbies safe, all over Miami shop owners and restaurateurs found themselves with new clientele who were prone to their own type of hysteria that Dad seemed to always be rattling his newspaper over.

"Juanita's was machine gunned today. A block from the federal building, can you believe the nerve?" he said to Mom.

Sheila and I had become experts at interpreting his newspaper rattles and creases to know when it was appropriate for us to chime in and have a chance at being heard.

"Paula got shot?" Sheila asked with grave concern.

"Who's Paula?" I asked.

One glare from Mom, and Dad realized it was not dinner conversation.

"Juanita's is—was, a great restaurant downtown—some bad guys didn't like who was eating inside," Dad said.

Night after night, it was always something, because when Castro took over Cuba, the smart Cubans (or at least the ones with money, according to Dad) fled for their lives, and Miami was the closest place to go. That, on top of the fact that organized crime the likes of mobsters seen in movies loved any chance to vacation in Miami, so the meeting of the crooked minds usually ended in someone getting hurt—or even killed. Mom was all over this, being from New York and with her "gift," she had their number—she could spout things that Dad could not find in the paper if he wrote it himself. So, no matter how much she wanted to keep the dinner conversation clean, we usually left the table knowing the whereabouts of some guy named Sam Giancana, but we couldn't tell our Cuban friends when their husbands and fathers would be back.

To make matters worse, my tutoring provided just enough knowledge for my friends and their mothers to be freaked out by the near daily headlines calling out "invasion teams"—mostly made up of Cuban renegades, too late to join the legitimate government-backed training. So, they used dilapidated boats and drove the US officials crazy in having to stop their explosives from tearing up our once-idyllic beach community.

Of course, I was at a loss because the schoolbooks I used for tutoring were outdated by Lincoln's standards, much less the reality of what we were facing as a community, state, and country. Still, I could not stop thinking about the entire country when my new best friends did not even have a country to call home, or a father to put a roof over their heads. Dad tried to make me feel better by explaining that our friends were the lucky ones: they got out of Cuba before their homes could be taken over.

"It's not easy for any of us, Roni, but I gotta tell ya, they are in the best possible scenario of all their friends who didn't make it out," Dad said.

"I don't understand why someone would want to take control of a country if it meant all of the country's people would be looking for a way to escape," I said to Dad in a rare moment when we were left alone. I loved those moments: a minute with Den was worth a life of cure.

All that said, to this day, a hurricane is the most dangerous thing about Florida. They are sneaky bastards, too; we can go years without a major storm, so we all let our guard down and then, *wham*, the entire population is on the sinking end of a rowboat with one oar to get out. Sure, there is plenty of warning a storm is coming, but hurricanes are so volatile that nobody knows for sure where it will hit—until it does. And the thing about people who have lived in Florida for any reasonable amount of time is that they think they can defy nature. They armor up for mosquitoes and sun. They know where to find a gator. They know what snakes they should go after with a shovel and how to swim in a riptide while avoiding jellyfish, sharks, and algae. So how much of a challenge can a little wind and rain be?

# CHAPTER 16

September of 1960, the hurricane storm chasers did not have any better technology than the residents had just by looking out a window. We all embraced hurricane Donna on September 2, but she decided to hang around for an unprecedented nine days.

The first day was business as usual, I had my ducks in a row, and we navigated to and from school with books and papers in plastic bags, and our sandals were easily kicked off to splash in puddles on the way home. The next day was the day before Labor Day break, so school was pointless. But parents like my mom needed us to be out of their hair so they could get to the store and take care of business before the storm and the holiday. Mom always put on a huge pot of homemade soup of beef and chunks of fresh vegetables, so we had food for a week we could heat up on the barbecue grill. We kept the soup in the pot on blocks of ice dad brought home from the Royal Ice Company on South Dixie Highway on his way back from the station. Dad was at the firehouse around the clock during times like this, which made Mom extra regimented and anxious. I will have to say that my mom, Dorothy, was strong. She always had to hold down the fort during disasters as my dad was ordered to go to the station. She was fearless so I believed, but I know now she had no choice.

As I walked my responsibilities home from school, it was quickly apparent that we were not going to make it without a life raft. The rain was brutal, I can honestly say, I have never felt rain hurt until then, or in the decades of hurricanes since. I could not imagine how the younger kids felt. Sure, they had storms in Cuba, but here they were in a new country, with a new language, and short one parent each. One little girl named Caridad, just stopped, and dropped as if she were practicing our school bomb drill. She was only six, and she barely spoke on a sunny day. With the rain so loud, I would not have heard her if she did scream. Sheila, who was usually my rear point person, had fallen out of position to run under the trees and lessen the sting of the pounding rain. I had an idea to go to Mrs. Achterkirch's house, as she lived at the bottom of the street closest to the school. I turned around to tell everyone and saw this little mound, dressed in white crouched in the middle of the sidewalk about half a block behind everyone. I yelled to Lourdes to steer them all to Mrs. Achterkirch's, and I ran back to get poor little Caridad.

Her jet-black hair stuck to her face, with the sand and pebbles the rain washed onto the sidewalk. I put her on my back and leaned into the rain, running as fast as my pigeon toes would allow in a torrential rainstorm.

Mrs. Achterkirch ushered us all in without question. I remember looking down at her floor and seeing how much of a puddle we brought in with us, thinking it was my responsibility to clean things up. But there was so much tension that the water that caused it became the least of our concerns.

Pablo, a chubby boy who played by the books, caught a glimpse of Mario watching me help Mrs. Achterkirch and called him on it.

"Mario likes Veronica," he said.

Mario grabbed Pablo by the throat as if he had been a lizard; he shoved him up against the wall causing Mrs. Achterkirch's pictures to wobble and fall.

It was scary. Mrs. Achterkirch did not say a word, she just pushed through the soggy kids and yanked Mario by the hair, pulling him off Pablo's throat.

"In my house, everyone lives free or dies," she whispered.

Mario was more freaked out by this than he could be by any blood-licking lizard. So, he backed off and shut up for the rest of the afternoon, maybe even the week.

"I'm so sorry, I kept hoping it would let up some for me to get to them sooner," Mom said. We all filed toward the door and prepared for the mad dash to her car. "I hope they weren't too much trouble."

"Bah, I tied up the bad ones, so it was no problem," Mrs. Achterkirch said, cracking herself up.

As we left, Lourdes whispered to me that "she could use paint to brighten the place up," I happened to look up and catch Mrs. Achterkirch eye-to-eye. I felt horrible about that for a long time after, even though it was not me who said it.

That night Dad was still at the station, and the TV was nothing but static no matter how much Mom fiddled with the rabbit ears. Even so, Sheila and I sat in our pajamas on the floor with our eyes glued to it – waiting for a miracle.

"I don't know how your father does this," Mom said as she tweaked the metal rods every which way.

"Figures, we don't have school tomorrow Dad's not here to hog TV and we can't get a picture," I said. I was moping, not because the TV was fuzzy, and not so much because the rain would not stop, but because it was the day before my birthday. It was sure to be ruined by Hurricane Donna—that fact was certainly clear. I was born on Labor Day, September 5, 1951, and hurricanes always took my breath away.

"Well, at least we have power," Mom said. "How about story time?"

# CHAPTER 17

"Shut up!" I was so upset, Sheila's stupid comment made me snap. I jumped up and smacked the rabbit ears out of my way. In some bizarre way, Jackie Kennedy was our hurricane miracle. She did a commercial for her husband's presidential campaign in perfectly fluent Spanish. This was 1960, and there was no Univision or even any Spanish radio stations. But it was clear the would-be first lady knew what she was doing. The three of us stood frozen until it registered that she was speaking in another language and that it was not the TV acting weird.

"Oh, she's smart," Mom said.

By the time Dad made it home, Hurricane Donna had dumped over ten inches of rain, and President Eisenhower had declared Miami a disaster area. We ran out front to greet him. The rain had stopped, I thought, but we were getting sprayed from everything that was soaked. Dad started to pick up trash can lids and the odd things that got jammed into bushes or blown down the street. I was helping him turn up a planter when we spotted something pink in the hedges. Our eyes connected; we both knew it was my bike. Dad pulled it out, the frame was bent, and it had some rust, probably from before the storm.

"I'm sorry your birthday is a washout," he said.

"Mom said I could have a rain check."

Dad laughed out loud and winked at Mom.

"Well, it seemed appropriate," she said.

Just then we heard a scream coming from down the block. It sounded like someone was being murdered.

Dad hopped up. "You girls stay here, I'll look."

He followed the commotion to find it coming from Mario's house. We followed Dad, and as soon as he stopped, we stepped far enough back to still see what was going on but not to be noticed by Dad or the murderer. They had their windows open, and we could hear the news talking about Castro visiting America. Another scream came from upstairs, and Dad slowly approached the front door.

Suddenly, a small TV came flying out of the upstairs window, forcing Dad to duck and cover. When he saw what it was, he picked up the TV and carried it to the front door.

"I don't care how upset someone is, you don't throw a perfectly good television out of your window," Mom said.

Dad did not get a chance to knock when the door flung open and Mario charged out in a fury. Dad quickly put the TV down and caught Mario in his arms. The boy was so hysterical he could not even put up a fight; instead, he broke down in tears.

I started to go help, but Mom pulled me back.

"I'm old enough to fight for my country. I want Castro dead! He's on holiday while my dad is—"

Mario broke down in breathless sobs, and Dad hugged him until he calmed down.

When the time was right, Dad let him come up for air, and a string of slobber broke between them. "You know, I never let Veronica slobber on me," Dad said.

"She's very pretty, I doubt she slobbers much," Mario said.

I gasped as Sheila giggled, and Mom shushed us both. "Come on girls, let the boys work it out."

I peeked back as we went home and saw Dad and Mario talking and tossing a football.

"Told ya, Mario loves Veronica," Sheila said.

"He probably won't when your father gets done with him," Mom said. Your dad played for the University of Kentucky until he was drafted. The 1945 college football season finished with the undefeated US Military Academy, more popularly known as "Army," being the unanimous choice for the national number-one team by the 116 voters in the Associated Press writers' poll. When dad was drafted the Army placed him at halfback for the Army football team playing football through WWII.

I wasn't sure if it was because Dad was going to tell him to stay away from me or because he was going to spread more lies about me, but I will always remember that last bit of chaos after the storm when Mario revealed his darkest self to Dad. I felt a new kind of sorry for these families. What kind of training could be so secret that they were allowed no contact with their fathers, sons, and brothers? It was also the first time I wondered if Dad was sorry that he had two girls and no sons.

I did not know much about Fidel Castro, other than he took over Cuba. But after Mario snapped, I started to pay even more attention to Dad's papers and news programs. Mario was now a permanent fixture at our front door, always wanting Dad to come out and play. Mom would tease Dad about it, like he was a little boy who had to "not wander off, stay off of Mrs. Achterkirch' lawn, and be sure and to be back for supper and wash his hands." We got a good laugh out of it, but underneath the teasing, we could all see that Dad loved to have someone to toss the football around with. I had to be careful about even watching them, because anytime I was within earshot of Mario, Sheila would bring up the idea that he was in love with me and was just using Dad to get to me. Anyway, I still had to see to it that he got to and from school every day. And given that Mario was such a know-it-all, I made a point to learn as much as I could about Castro.

Soon enough, the news about this guy Castro was everywhere. First, during that visit to New York, that Mario flipped the TV channel when he heard that a little girl was gunned down in a restaurant where someone thought Castro was dining. With this coming after Juanita's restaurant shootout, I told Mom I never wanted to eat out again.

# CHAPTER 18

I volunteered to take the kids trick-or-treating around the neighborhood when Halloween rolled around. I dressed as a scarecrow; it was the only use I had for the flannel shirt that my grandma in New York sent me. Sheila was an angel, and Lourdes was a princess, and another boy, Marco, was a cowboy. I am sure there is a well-funded study somewhere that points out how people dress as their true personalities on Halloween, but one look at our lineup could have saved the trouble.

Lourdes and I had prepped her grandma on how to hand out treats when someone knocked, so we decided to test her.

"I feel so American," Marco said as we waited for her to answer with our sacks open.

We could hear her singing to the TV commercials inside. "*Es Kennedy, Kennedy, Kennedy for President...*" she sang.

Lourdes pointed to Mario lurking up in the tree in her yard just as Grandma opened the door.

"*Ay, que linda,*" Grandma said as she plunked caramel apples into our bags.

"If America is so great, why do you have to beg for treats?" Mario wondered. He was lurking in a tree that bordered the street.

Grandma hurled a caramel apple at him, causing him to lose his balance and fall to the ground. He was fine; in fact, he landed like he meant to do it. He laughed and ate the apple.

The only thing to keep me from being sucked into the drama of our personal little Havana community was the drama being played out in the news. It got to the point that Dad would have the paper to his nose, with the TV news on and the kitchen radio playing news all at the same time.

"You know they all have the same source," Mom told him. "And you can bet they all exaggerate for the sake of their wallets."

Dad would just let her vent. Occasionally he let her have her way and put music on the radio. But even then, he would push her buttons and make her tell him what she thought the day's biggest story would be.

"Come on, now," he said. "You always say that your intuition is the most reliable source."

"Alright," she said, flipping her hair back and squaring her shoulders. "I say it's only a matter of time until someone squeals about this so-called training they have all these Cuban men doing, and the whole operation is going to blow up leaving out the next President in hornet's nest and these poor people with no chance in hell of ever seeing home again."

"Mom said a bad word," Sheila blurted from our eaves-dropping place.

I was too hung up on the other words Mom said to hush her. We were busted. The next day, the news was back on the kitchen radio while we ate breakfast.

*Mobster Sam Giancana is pulling no punches when it comes to getting the CIA off his back; he has blown the cover of the top-secret Cuba Project. Stating that hundreds of Cuban Nationals have been secretly training in a military camp in Homestead, Florida. The mob boss claims to have been in touch with the family of the boy who was mistakenly killed by the recruits when he threw a firecracker over the fence of the Homestead camp. It sounded like gunfire. It may be too soon to say whether the mob boss's tactic will work in getting the feds to leave him alone, but surely someone has some explaining to do. More to come as this unfolds...*

Mom stood in front of Dad with a hot pot of coffee ready to pour into his cup, she shot him the *I told you so* look that mothers do so well. He laughed and gave her a hug.

"I never doubted you for a second."

She knew he was full of it but let him off easy. "Tip of the iceberg, mark my words," she said.

Just as we were finishing breakfast there was a pounding at the door. Mom looked out the window and saw Mario on the front step. "Veronica see what he needs," she said.

"He probably wants to play ball with Dad," I said.

She shot me her *I did not ask for your opinion* look, so I went to the door. Before I had it open all the way, he barged in frantically looking for my dad.

"Take me," he cried. "It's nearby, I want to go. I want to fight."

Dad had to explain to him that he had no access to the training camp in Homestead, and if Mario had been older, they would have taken him with the others. He had to go about this same thing about ten different ways before Mario calmed down and let up on his demands.

Dad knew where the Cuban men went for training, but he did not want to get into the details with Mario. In April 1960, the CIA began to recruit anti-Castro Cuban exiles in the Miami area. Until July 1960, assessment and training were carried out on USEPA Island located on Florida's southwest Gulf coast between Sarasota and Naples, and at various secret facilities in south Florida, such as found on the Homestead Airforce Base.

The Nixon and Kennedy debates leading up to the election were fascinating to the adults, but we kids got tired of the same old arguments, none of us could understand why the election process was still going on—why couldn't they just have a vote and be done with it? Surprisingly, Sheila kept us entertained with her incredible impression of Nixon. She had this way of shaking her chubby cheeks and slurring her voice just enough to really nail his personality. So as Dad followed his news like a gambler following the races, she would shadow him quoting Nixon's refusal to comment on plans for Cuba. As the election was finally upon us, Mom had her do it one more time.

"It's not that I think he's going away, but I don't think we'll hear from him for a while," Mom said.

Sheila stood in front of the TV, spread her feet apart, and somehow forced the chub of her cheeks to sag. "I am not at liberty to discuss ongoing efforts," she said. Her Nixon impersonation was so cute and realistic.

We all laughed, and Dad got even more excited when the news broke in with the first election returns. Kennedy was in the lead.

We awoke to a party of presidential proportions. Kennedy had won, and the Cubans in Miami were certain he would help them reunite with their country and families. The city exploded with pop-up parties and parades. Once again, Dad manned the grill for a community block party. We all quieted down to listen to his acceptance speech over Dad's radio. Dad was also a pro at running extension cords up the wall inside, so his radio could perch on the windowsill as he worked outside.

*Every degree of mind and spirit I possess will be devoted to the long-range interest of the United States and to the cause of freedom around the world.*

Kennedy said a lot more, but I remember that line as the moment that all our Cuban neighbors breathed a sigh of relief; some even blessed themselves.

As the burgers and dogs all settled in our gullets and Dad helped we kids roast marshmallows, Mrs. Achterkirch blurt out something about a lame duck, and Mom had to explain to the Cuban ladies that even though Kennedy won, it wouldn't be until New Year's that he could actually start the job.

# CHAPTER 19

Before his inauguration, John F. Kennedy was briefed on a plan by the CIA developed in the Eisenhower administration to train Cuban exiles for an invasion of their homeland. The plan anticipated that the Cuban people and elements of the Cuban military would support the invasion.

Lourdes's mom was the first to do the math and realize that this meant the men would miss Christmas with their families. Silent tears streamed down her round, tan cheeks as Lourdes brought her a toasted marshmallow. Before Lourdes could ask *que?* her grandma had pulled her and her mom toward the gate to go home.

It was clear that our neighbors were not the only ones in Miami concerned with how long it seemed to be taking the Cuban recruits to take action, especially now that the project was not so secret anymore. Soon, local churches started funding flights out of Cuba to Miami for children whose parents were promised they would be able to follow. I did not understand the politics or the rules, but apparently the families still in Cuba were clamoring to get out, but the families in Florida wanted nothing more than to go back. The problem was, they did not want to go back with this guy Castro in charge, and Castro would not let the adults out of Cuba. But he was more than happy to get rid of the kids. This is how the Pedro Pan operation started. Parents in Cuba were certain that their children would be better off parentless in a strange land than with their parents in a Cuba being run by a ruthless man prone to extreme behavior.

I overheard Mrs. Achterkirch telling Mom that Father O'Donnell was coordinating foster homes for the children. I could not imagine there were too many more neighborhoods like ours who had girls like me to help even more kids get acclimated to life in Florida. This was a month before Kennedy took office. As Christmas neared, the Pedro Pan flights were all over the news. The children were being put up in a camp near the Homestead training camp until foster homes could be assigned.

"Isn't that where the boy was killed because of a firecracker?" I asked.

"It was a horrible accident," Dad said.

"I sure hope none of them brought cap guns," Mom said.

"How many guests can America hold?" Sheila asked.

Mom had lost patience. "Find a Christmas show, please, or turn it off altogether."

"But I thought everyone could go home if he won President?" Sheila was not quite ready to end the conversation.

# CHAPTER 20

They were saved by the bell—the one that meant Mom's Christmas cookies were done.

"I want you girls to take some Christmas cookies to Mrs. Achterkirch," Mom said.

"But she's Jewish." It was my turn to question the adult logic.

"She can still have cookies, come on," Mom said.

As we walked to Mrs. Achterkirch, Mario jumped out and scared us. Technically Sheila's scream scared me, but either way I struggled to hang on to the platter of cookies. Mario twirled his football and laughed.

"How come your dad never taught you to throw a football?"

He pushed a button that I had rather never got activated, but I managed to keep it together as I eyed Mrs. Achterkirch's house ahead.

"Who says he didn't? Come on, Sheila."

"Chicken," Mario said.

"Lizard." It was the best I could come up with.

We were in such a hurry to get up to Mrs. Achterkirch's door, I did not notice the car parked out front. The same fancy car that led the Cuban caravan into the neighborhood. Inside, it took me a minute to place the man as the same guy because he was with a young Cuban boy. I thought he was the boy's dad, but I should have known that was not possible. I was not really thinking about stuff like that.

That was the first time I met Carlos, the same guy who dropped me off to watch my father die. He was a frightened little boy with big brown eyes pawing the small photo frames Mrs. Achterkirch had on her coffee table.

"If you want to live here" She stood over Carlos and I'm sure he thought, same as me, that the pause after "live," was just a little too long.

"You will not touch my memories. If they break, I will break."

Both Sheila and I were as wide eyed as the frightened little boy. Years later we would talk about her photos—all black and white, all from Germany—some from Dachau. We never went near them. But looking back, I think she would have liked to tell us about them.

Mario had snuck in the open door behind us as Mrs. Achterkirch introduced Sheila and me to Carlos.

"Veronica helps the Cuban children with their schoolwork," she said.

"Hola, Carlos," I said. "Where is your house? *Donde esta su cabeza?*" I tried to show off what little Spanish I knew to make him feel comfortable, but he stared at me funny.

"His head is right in front of you, thinking you're crazy," Mario said.

"Carlos is staying with me until his parents arrive from Cuba," Mrs. Achterkirch explained.

Mario said, "Let me help you with your Spanish, Veronica. When you want to make friends say *frotarse en las nalgas*."

I did not know what he said, but Carlos's jaw dropped, and Mrs. Achterkirch told Mario to go home. Saying *rubbing your buttocks* to a stranger was Mario's way of getting even. In those days during the Cuban American integration, American kids could not bank on an accurate translation due to colloquialism and visa versa.

Carlos was a Pedro Pan child who was taken in by Mrs. Achterkirch. Maybe it was because I was the first child he met after landing in this strange place, or maybe it was Mario's boldness that scared him and made me feel sorry for him, but after that night we shared a closer bond than I did with any of the other Cuban children in my care.

You can bet when January rolled around, we had as many people over to our house as it could fit to listen to President John F. Kennedy's famous inaugural speech. "A celebration of freedom," he called it. Thinking about it today, I cannot help but wonder if all presidential speeches would be more memorable if they were titled.

Lourdes's Grandma sat inches from the TV like she had never seen one, but we all knew she had it on every day at their house. Mom made Dad move his armchair up close so she would be comfortable. He protested at first, until Mom pulled him aside.

"She sits on that floor for an hour, she's liable to end up sleeping there she'll be so stiff," Mom said.

I do not know why my mom was so insistent on their comfort; they had been to parties at our house a bunch of times where it was everyone fending for themselves. I guess because she felt their comfort was tied to the new beginning for our country and theirs. As Lourdes and I translated for her mom, my mom offered her Avon.

"Elsa, this is for you... it's the latest thing all us gals are using."

I caught Dad rolling his eyes. He was not crazy about the Avon business model. Mom drove to various neighborhoods and parked the car with Sheila and me inside. She could not leave us home or pay for a babysitter, as the cost would eat into her profits. We would walk up to the door and call out, "Avon Lady!" Sheila and I giggled hysterically, and Mom gave us the evil eye.

Lourdes opened some nail polish and did her mom's nails, and everyone was happy.

As President Kennedy's voice became more passionate, Grandma clapped with every sentence. By the time he uttered his now-famous, "Ask not what your country can do for you, but what you can do for your country," Grandma was hugging everyone while crying tears of joy. Somehow, she understood what Kennedy meant, even when Lourdes did not.

"What does that mean? They sound the same," she said.

After I thought about it, I told her it meant that it was our responsibility to help our country. But Grandma put it more clearly.

"*Libertad*," she said. Florida was delirious. Cubans lit anything with a fuse and tooted and banged anything that made a sound. It was their New Year's Eve and Independence Day all in one.

# CHAPTER 21

We could hear the pop of firecrackers outside. We all left breakfast on the table and hurried outside to see our neighbors and friends run into the streets as if they could see the battle from there.

"What should we do, Dad?" I asked. "Let them enjoy this moment they are free now," he said.

We looked down the street and Mario waved to us. He had a wide smile. It was the first time I had ever seen him like that.

He ran up the sidewalk and shouted to us, "They did it! We're going home!"

"Are they going home now?" Sheila asked.

"That's the plan," Dad answered.

I could feel my fried egg rolling around in my belly. I lost my friends and my job all at once.

I remember seeing Mrs. Achterkirch with Carlos on her lawn and thinking, *That's got to be the shortest foster care experience ever.*

"How about I dust off your bike?" Dad said. He must have seen me turning green.

"Tire's flat," was all I could manage to say. I guess it was then that it hit me. If they left, I would be back to being pigeon-toed Veronica with the pink bike and plastic white basket. Not that this was a bad thing. I missed my bike, but it somehow seemed smaller, like an outfit I had outgrown, and I certainly had never lost a job before.

Mom picked up on my conundrum straight away. "I don't need to remind you about the best laid plans, do I?" she whispered to me.

I do not remember answering. Sheila went off on a rambling series of questions as the neighbors' celebration grew. Mom probably knew we needed a focus; we could not just gape at them all day.

"Let's do something special for them, for all of us, an all-American send off," she said.

By lunch she had it all figured out. We would take the whole street bowling, and as an extra surprise, we would go for manicures beforehand at the salon next to the bowling alley with Lourdes, her grandma, and her mother. Dad thought this was silly, because the nails would get messed up when they stuck their hands in the balls, but he knew better than to push it when Mom was saving the day.

Lourdes got into a Cuban flurry of words where I could only pick up things like "Cuba" and "Libre." I pulled out a *LIFE* magazine that had the Statue of Liberty on the cover, and I explained to them that our country was about liberty.

"I am going to work in Washington, DC, when I grow up," I said.

Mom, Dad, and even Sheila stopped and looked my way. I had never made a proclamation of my adult goals before, and I guess it surprised them; I know it surprised me.

"I thought you wanted to be free from helping Cubans so you could be free to ride your bike?" Sheila asked.

It would have been easier to ignore if it were not at the exact moment the station paused waiting for a commercial to start. The room was silent.

Grandma, Lourdes, and any other Cuban who spoke a lick of English seemed to squirm and look for their bags to go home.

"You're such a child," I said.

Poor Sheila broke down in tears, and the party broke up. I stewed long and hard that night and decided that if my mouth spurted out that I wanted to work in DC, then it must be a sign, and I decided to work even harder at helping our Cuban neighbors figure out their own liberty.

"*Ding dong*, it's Mario," Sheila sang. Mario's habit of calling on Dad to play football had become so chronic that every time the doorbell rang, Sheila sang.

"I hope that's Avon calling," Mom said as she searched the junk drawer for the hundredth time. "I can't find my nail polish anywhere... not like I can run to Winn Dixie and get some because now it's a Sedano's... "

"I'll get it," I said.

"*Ding dong*, it's Mario."

"Are you getting it today?" Mom asked.

"I meant, I'll get the nail polish," I said. "I gave it to Lourdes to touch up her mom's nails."

Mom shot her with a *when were you going to tell me after I have wasted an hour looking?* glare.

"She's been really depressed; it's been months since the president took office, and the men still have not been heard from."

Mom let it go and flung open the door. "Now you've made me feel like a witch."

Mario looked at her with wide eyes. "No. If you were a witch, I would have left a chicken liver on your step and ran," he said.

Mom did not bother asking what he was talking about. I hurried past Mario as Mom turned back inside. We both said, "Dad's not home," and left him standing with the ball.

We heard nothing until April 1961. Even though we do not have the normal change of seasons in Florida, the feeling that spring brings still penetrates the atmosphere, probably because it is just before the humidity level creeps into the 90 percentiles. Whatever the reason, the feeling across South Florida was a palpable buzz. Cuban refugees seemed to be creating their own sense of nervousness that something had to happen soon. Then President Kennedy visited Palm Beach, about an hour north of Miami. He brought the family there for Easter along with a ton of security that was not the norm for a president at the time. According to Dad's news, there were threats on the family and rumors of kidnapping their little daughter, Caroline.

- CHAPTER 21 -

The Cuban population fed off the buzz and almost willed something to happen, with signs popping up all over Miami that read: "Cuba Libre."

Then one day at breakfast, it was Mom's turn at music on the radio. It was interrupted.

That is when reality set in, and the horrible news was broadcast. April 13, 1961, the largest-ever trained CIA brigade launched an attack on Cuba. That brigade was made up of the Cuban men who had been training for over a year without seeing their families. It is finally happening Fidel Castro is going to be overthrown.

The original plan called for two air strikes against Cuban air bases. A 140-man invasion force would disembark under cover of darkness and launch a surprise attack. Paratroopers dropped out of the sky before the invasion to disrupt transportation and repel Cuban forces. Simultaneously, a smaller force would land on the east coast of Cuba to create confusion.

89

# CHAPTER 22

The main force would advance across the island to Matanzas to set up a defensive position. The URF (United Revolutionary Front) would send leaders to south Florida to establish a temporary government. The success of the plan depended on the Cuban population joining the invaders.

The first calamity occurred on April 15. Eight bombers departed from Nicaragua to bomb the Cuban airfields. The CIA used B-26 bombers from World War II. They were obsolete. They painted them like Cuban air force planes. The bombers missed most of their targets, leaving Castro's air force intact. The news featured the repainted bombers on TVs across the nation, and Kennedy cancelled the second strike. He was probably worried about how he looked to the eyes of the world.

On April 17, the Cuban-exiled invasion force, known as Brigade 2506, landed on beaches along the Bay of Pigs. They were under very heavy fire without American back-up. The Cuban air force attacked the invaders, sank two escort ships, and destroyed half the exiles' air support. Bad weather hampered the ground force. They were left with soggy equipment and insufficient ammo. Castro ordered twenty thousand troops to advance to the beach, and the Cuban air force ruled the skies.

President Kennedy authorized an "air umbrella" at dawn on April 19. Six unmarked American fighter planes took off to help the brigade's B-26 aircraft. However, the "Cuban" B-26 arrived late, confused by the change in time zones between Nicaragua and Cuba. Castro's air force shot them down, and the invasion was over.

Some exiles escaped to the sea, while the rest were killed or rounded up and imprisoned by Castro's soldiers. Almost twelve hundred members of Brigade 2506 surrendered, and more than a hundred were killed.

Castro's infamous firing squads known as "El Paradon" (The Wall) did not discriminate. Black and white, old, and young, rich, and poor were sent to the wall and executed. Anyone that disagreed with Castro and his gang were murdered. Castro set up a firing squad and lined up his childhood friends and members of his baseball team, killing them all for being traitors to the Revolution. Mario's father was the pitcher on the same baseball team as Castro, and he was killed that day by the firing squad.

So many exile soldiers were killed due to the botched air strike stranding the brave Cuban men who got their families out safely and went back to fight for their country at the Bay of Pigs.

While the attack was not public yet, Dad took our neighbors bowling to cheer them up. The Colosseum

Bowling Alley was about as 1950s as you could get, but even so the lights, sounds, and scoreboards had our friends in awe. Dad helped Mario, Marco, and a couple other boys perfect their roll, while Mrs. Achterkirch proved his methods inadequate as she instructed Carlos. We "ladies" escaped to the salon next door before Dad had a chance to stop us.

Mom and Elsa really bonded as they giggled to each other about one of the hairdressers who was popping out of her uniforms.

"I can't believe we didn't do this sooner," Mom said.

Lourdes translated for her mother who let off a flurry of Spanish, only for Lourdes to come back and say, "Yes."

We laughed at that for another twenty minutes, giggling with our traditional Cuban glittered faces and hands as we skittered back to the lanes. It was dark outside, and Lourdes and I felt like teenagers staying out past curfew. Lipstick will do that to young girls toying with new hormones. We stepped up to our lanes in time to see both Dad and Mrs. Achterkirch throw strikes. You could see the competition between them was set, even if it were in good fun. I got the feeling Dad would cave to Mrs. Achterkirch's scare tactics (which were nothing more than well-calculated looks).

They nodded to each other, and we all turned to see the goofy monitor graphics that pop up when someone does something good. But our screen was black. All the screens were. We looked around confused. Dad calmed us and indicated that a cursor was blinking on the screen.

# Chapter 23

The headline scrolled on one painful letter at a time until we all read the white on black text like it was a computer telex from Mars:

U.S. Fails. Defeated in Bay of Pigs

Time stood still for what seemed like ten minutes. Then Dad put down his ball and took off his shoes.

"I better call into work," he said.

I wiped my cherry lip-gloss off. If Dad was showing up at the fire department on his night off, it was serious enough to not wear fruity lacquer on my lips. But at the same time the ache in the pit in my stomach that had been there all day was gone. The details and consequences of what happened in the Bay of Pigs would take decades to unravel. I had no way of knowing that, but I did know I had a renewed sense of purpose when Dad told me to help gather up everyone's bowling shoes. I stepped into my responsibility as if I were just rehired with a promotion. I knew not to smile, but I felt lighter and happier than I had all day. My job helping these Cuban families was not a job at all: they had become a part of my life, and I was happy they were staying.

As we made our way home, Lourdes wondered aloud whether this meant that the men could come home. We all looked to Dad for an answer; he looked to Mom who stiffened and reached for a cigarette.

"It's too soon to know what will happen next," Dad said. We drove home in silence.

# CHAPTER 24

Brigade 2506, the paramilitary group that led the Bay of Pigs invasion force, took its name from the serial number of one of its members. Early in 1960, President Dwight D. Eisenhower authorized the CIA to recruit Cuban exiles living in Miami and train them for an invasion of Cuba.

Cuban leader Fidel Castro (1926–2016) established the first Communist state in the Western Hemisphere after leading an overthrow of the military dictatorship of Fulgencio Batista in 1959. He ruled over Cuba for nearly five decades, until handing off power to his younger brother.

According to many historians, the CIA and the Cuban exile brigade believed that President Kennedy would eventually allow the American military to intervene in Cuba on their behalf. However, the president was resolute: as much as he did not want to "abandon Cuba to the communists," he said, he would not start a fight that might end in World War III. His efforts to overthrow Castro never flagged. In November 1961, he approved Operation Mongoose, an espionage and sabotage campaign to instigate a revolt to overthrow the Communist regime within Cuba and institute a new government with which the United States could live in peace. Exploding cigars and detonation devices in Castro's shoes were just a couple of devices used to try to kill Castro. But he never went so far as to provoke an outright war. In 1962, the Cuban Missile Crisis further inflamed American Cuban-Soviet tensions.

It was announced in a TV address on October 22, 1962, during the Cuban Missile Crisis, that leaders of the United States and the Soviet Union engaged in a tense, thirteen-day political and military standoff in October 1962 over the installation of Soviet nuclear missiles on Cuba, just ninety miles from US shores.

Over the next couple of days, we learned just how badly the Bay of Pigs mission went. President Kennedy was blamed for leading the men into an ambush that left no survivors. Not only were my friends not going back to Cuba, they would never see their fathers and husbands again. From that time on, the children of Miami and all nationalities had to live in a culture of fear and espionage.

Mom told me that the kids needed routine, so they did not have to think to get through their days. So, the next week I had Lourdes help me with the rations like she used to do, and Sheila and I made a point to get the kids and hang out at the field after dinner. It was not much, but simple things like counting stars and listening to toads seemed to allow us time together without having to say too much. Mrs. Achterkirch did her best to keep the kids occupied, too. Lourdes's mom Elsa was in a big funk. By the end of the week there was no sign she had ever been to a salon.

One day when Carlos was walking home from my house after a tutoring session, arms full of books, he was shocked to see Mario come barreling out his front door as if the house was on fire.

"He's coming for us!"

His mom did not come after him but stood behind the screen door and blessed herself.

"Tell her!" Mario jumped at the first person he saw: Carlos.

Carlos dropped his books and Mario attacked him.

I heard something from inside and ran out to see Mrs. Achterkirch pulling Mario off a traumatized Carlos. I ran to help. Mrs. Achterkirch pulled Mario's arms behind him and I kicked him—right where it hurts. His mom finally stepped out and helped him hobble inside, while we picked up Carlos's books.

"They're coming back, it's a cover up," Mario cried.

Mrs. Achterkirch made a comment about their being nothing wrong with my legs. I felt bad, telling Mrs. Achterkirch that it was pure instinct that kicked in. She laughed at my joke and took us for flan. We had never tasted flan before the Cubans came to town, and we all loved it with the caramel custard with a layer of hard caramel on top. It was a great diversion.

Downtown Miami was in total chaos. I think this was the first time I really noticed how much it had changed since Cubans had started coming in. Little shops and cafés had popped up with signs selling Cuban goods in

Spanish. "Cuba Libre" signs were everywhere. People were on edge. This was no longer the beach community I knew; it was a little scary, but more exciting than anything. To me it was new, and we did not have to move It was like an emotion-driven circus came to town and never left.

As time went on, I noticed how much English Lourdes and her grandmother learned from watching television, and I convinced my parents to let me have a TV night for the kids in the neighborhood as a part of my tutoring. Dad ended up using the time to play football with Mario and sometimes other boys, but as he said, "It was all educational, these boys needed to understand how competition works in America." After all, dad was a University of Kentucky star halfback and the children aroused his love of the game. How a game of football can make men boys again is beyond me.

# CHAPTER 25

On February 14, everyone stayed in our living room, glued to the TV for Jackie Kennedy's White House tour. It helped that Dad was working late, so the boys had no one to coach them.

When Dad did come in, he had gifts for Valentine's Day. Dad always stopped at the Rexall Drug Store to buy huge heart-shaped boxes of chocolate for Mom and us girls. The chocolate was not that great, but we did not know better in the early days. We knew Dad loved us so much, and when he made special trips home from the station, we knew he was showing his love.

He slipped into the house with his prizes praising the first lady of the house for standing in for him. We barely acknowledged him. We were so glued to the set trying to imagine how the Kennedys lived. A cigarette commercial came on and Lourdes's grandma sung and clapped to the jingle like a five-year-old, making us all laugh.

"Tastes good like a... (*clap, clap*) cigarette should."

"I guess you've successfully Americanized them," Dad said to me. "But don't they have their own televisions?"

"You're the one who got her into this role," Mom said.

"Well I never thought she wouldn't get out."

When the next school year rolled around, I was in third grade at Fairlawn Elementary School. But many of the Cuban children were going to be held back because they did not understand or speak English. The standards for them to be in the grade that matched their age and school level were not really enforced the first year because nobody thought they would be here beyond that time. A few were being held back two years, so I had fifth graders in my third-grade classroom. The real issue was that these so-called kids were raised in a culture whereby the time they hit double digits, raging hormones were encouraged, even if they were not yet developed. It was difficult in the girls' bathroom to see to comb my hair. The Cuban girls were tall and beautiful. They had lots of confidence, and all I could do was watch and hope to get a glimpse of myself in a mirror. I loved watching them. They wore skinny belts under their full gathered skirts to ensure a small waist while maturing. My pudgy little body did not like tight belts, and Mom never mentioned how to maintain an hourglass figure.

Through our evening field talks, I learned that in Cuba, girls are chaperoned from the time they turned ten. The culture is passionate and sensual, and as early as the fifth grade, Cuban boys are taught to flex their "bravado" for the ladies. But in America, in the early sixties, elementary students were still reading about Dick and Jane, and you can bet Jane was always modestly dressed, acting like she had never heard of the word "sex" much less understood the act of it. Of course, when Nancy Drew popped into the picture, we loved watching her detective work in finding secret stairways behind bookcases. No boys were featured except in the Hardy Boys series, which as a tomboy, was my favorite.

Carlos, thanks to my tutoring and Mrs. Achterkirch's pragmatism, was not held back. Mario was. So here we had this somewhat timid and small Cuban eleven-year-old preparing for junior high and football, This should have been my first clue as to the diversity of the Cuban children as children are all over the world, but I was still too focused on figuring out the politics that Dad was so absorbed in.

# CHAPTER 26

The *Miami Herald* headlines were about the mob, Castro, and Kennedy, things I could sort of figure out and speak to the neighborhood kids about how they impacted our world. These were figures that seemed real and maybe not so threatening because we all could put a face to them and understood their roles. I accepted that Miami had grown up to be a little edgier and unpredictable. My Cuban friends had mostly accepted that this was their new home, and my parents accepted things that I could only hear if I eavesdropped and did not get caught.

Until one day, the school was blasted with air raid sirens. These were not our typical bell-ringing fire drills, these sirens were something none of us had ever heard or even knew existed.

My teacher caught her breath just as the duck and cover announcement came over the intercom speakers. We had practiced this drill just the week before but without the head-splitting sirens.

We all crouched under our desks; Carlos looked at me with cartoon-wide eyes. I could tell he was about to cry. I was focused on trying to calm him from across the room so when Mom's face leaned in, I jumped, as if she was a bear. I could not hear what she was saying, but her face was dead serious. She pulled me out, and I saw Sheila hanging on to her leg. She pulled both of us tight and hurried us out of the class. At least I had time to take down the flag.

"Wait!" I shouted. It became a tug of war of arms as I realized there was no way I was leaving these kids who had followed me like ducklings for almost a year. Mom finally understood, and in a matter of seconds, we pulled all the Cuban children on my street out from under their desks and ran to Mom's car.

Mom's car was packed with kids, but that did not stop her from chain smoking the whole way.

"The bombs are real?" I asked.

"The president is working on getting rid of them," Mom said.

"Fidel wants us all dead," Lourdes cried. "Cubans aren't safe anywhere."

"Where's Dad?" I asked.

"He's working."

I now had to add Russia to the news headline rotation. To me, all I could imagine were these angry Eskimo-like people who just wanted to take over someplace warm like Florida or Cuba, so they parked a ton of missiles off the coast until someone gave them a place to stay. But after hearing Mom talk to Dad when she thought we were sleeping, I learned that the Russians had bombs pointed at Florida and it was up to President Kennedy to convince them not to blow us to bits.

For thirteen days everyone in Florida jumped if a mosquito so much as farted. President Kennedy became resident Kennedy, living in Florida as he bargained for a miracle. In the end he was successful, and the missiles were removed, so they said, which made him like a god to me. I remember thinking, *How does someone train to talk their way out of a bomb threat without freaking out?* I reasoned with myself that presidents must have this ability.

Sadly, even though he saved us, the whole event reopened old wounds from the Bay of Pigs failure. Cubans trying to escape to America to meet up with their Pedro Pan children, and Cubans already in Florida hoping to return to their home country were stripped of hope and may as well have been hit with a missile. For the first time I noticed that some of the Cuban adults were not so nice to the American adults. Mom had stopped by Lourdes's to see if her mom wanted to go shopping with her. Elsa told her, through Lourdes's interpretation, "to get her priorities straight." Mrs. Achterkirch went over to Mario's house and offered to take him with Carlos to go to baseball tryouts, and Mario's mom spit on Mrs. Achterkirch. I did not see it, but Carlos told me that Mrs. A grabbed Mario's mom by the collar and made her apologize.

A few months later, President Kennedy was back in Miami to honor the men lost in the Bay of Pigs. This was not just a press conference, as the event filled the Orange Bowl with Cubans and Americans alike. A lot of the Pedro Pan children lived in a Catholic charities compound nearby and they all clamored to get in. If the president had lost support from the Cuban exiles after the fiasco, this event gained it all back.

"They cannot eliminate our determination to be free," he said. The crowd went wild. He honored every man lost, and every family in our neighborhood was mentioned. If this was not enough, when he was finished, Mrs. Kennedy got up and spoke for at least ten minutes in Spanish more perfect than Lourdes's. The jam-packed stadium hung on her every word. I had always aspired to be like JFK, but that moment, I shed the tomboy in me and thought aspiring to be Jackie would not be a bad thing.

Mom leaned in and whispered to me, "Stick with what you're good at, even I couldn't pull that off." Mom had a way of making non-minced words sound well intentioned. One thing is for sure, everyone got the truth whether they asked for it or not. I think that is what Dad saw in her originally, because he was a football-playing farm boy from Kentucky, and Mom; she was a street-smart firecracker from Manhattan who never told a lie. Dad used to joke that when he would call his parents to tell him about his girlfriend he always said, "She's an honest woman." Then he would hang up and joke with her that she left a wake of bruises in her path because the truth hurt so much.

Mom and Dad had the sort of relationship that old Humphrey Bogart movies are made of lots of quick quips and flirty glances until they could get each other alone.

Sheila and I caught them on more than one occasion, slow dancing and kissing much longer than parents normally do if they know kids are watching.

But Mom always knew. She'd act like she didn't and say something shocking to Dad like, "I've been thinking we should ship Veronica off to boarding school."

As Lourdes, Mario, Marco, Carlos, and I were supposed to get promoted to the fourth grade, we learned that Lourdes, Mario, and Marco were being held back. This was almost a blanket decision and based mostly on the language barrier. My friends did not come right out and blame me, but I could not help but feel that I failed them somehow. Carlos, who studied with me a lot, assured me it was not my fault—he was moving on after all. I felt the worst for Lourdes, as her English was rather good. We all walked home a little slower from school the day we found out. Sheila was bound to get home ahead of us since we were all talking in turmoil.

"What's that all about out there?" Mom asked her.

"School drama," Sheila said with a sigh. Sheila did not get involved in controversial situations. She saw through all the confusion. It was canny how she could predict things. Maybe she had mom's gift?

Lourdes and I were not two steps in the door when Mom chimed in. "The Cuban kids who pass the English test will be moving on to their age appropriate grade are going to be faced with a lot of changes when they reach Middle School, so they might as well stick to the books and adapt."

"I won't know until next year if my English will be good enough," Lourdes said.

When we explained what was going on, Mom was ready to spring into action. The next day she was in the school administrator's office for over an hour. I do not know exactly what she said, but Dad joked that she held him hostage until he agreed to test Lourdes. She took the test and could jump to junior high school.

It probably took almost a year but looking back all I can remember is that it was not too long after that I wished Mom never helped her.

As most drama goes, it all started with a kiss. Lourdes still wore the pretty white linen and embroidered dresses she wore from Cuba, but children grow a lot the last years of grade school, and her clothes were a bit snug. She was more developed than me. Hell, who am I kidding? *She was popping out of her linen like a college co-ed.* So, a lot of eyes were on her, and she liked the attention. We certainly did not have a falling out over her needing a bra, but there was a marked shift in how she carried herself. So, I began to step back and do my own thing. We met more Cuban children from outside our neighborhood, wealthier ones. And I think Lourdes felt entitled to be their friends.

Two brothers, only a year apart, were chauffeured by limo to school every day. Antonio and Alfredo Fernandez were the grandsons of Rafael Guas Inclan, the vice president of Cuba under Batista, and they were gorgeous even in junior high. One day, the chauffeur stopped me on my way into school and handed me a letter for my parents. All day long that thing burned a hole in my pocket. I could not imagine what it said. "You're moving up, sweetheart, we should double your price," Mom said. Apparently, the Fernandez brothers needed an American tutor. "I don't get paid to tutor," I said.

"Well, you should."

"Please don't embarrass me, they'll think we're poor."

"Oh, I'm just kidding. You show them who's boss."

I just rolled my eyes and left before she got any other bright ideas.

Soon enough, the limo started to bring the brothers to our neighborhood after school. The first day they could just hang out and play with us while the limo waited. Sheila and I had some grown-up sister bonding as we had to stop ourselves from staring at them. Mario showed them how to throw a football. He was all sweaty with his shirt off, which made us girls giggle even more. Lourdes made a comment in Spanish to get their attention. Antonio, the older one did not take the bait, but Alfredo laughed, and soon they were gone.

The next day the limo parked, and the brothers came to my house with their homework. When their homework was finished, Mom gave us some cookies for a snack. I remember thinking they were fancier than any cookies she normally bought. As I walked them to the limo, we could see the other kids up at the corner lot. Sheila waved, and as I waved back, Antonio grabbed my hand and kissed my cheek. Now mind you, even though I had been hanging around with Cubans, it was always me trying to help them feel like they belonged in America.

From the sounds of the kids up the street, I think they forgot on I was a mission not a romance. I heard Mario above all the others: "Blondie has a boyfriend."

In a blur, Antonio and Alfredo hopped into the limo, and I swooned back into the house, not caring what the kids were saying. That was my first kiss, even though it did not count since it was on my cheek. *A girl could dream.*

# CHAPTER 27

"Aren't they cute?" Sheila said to Lourdes. Lourdes did not answer, she just stared at the limo as it drove away. "Having Inclan as a grandfather has benefits," Tony said. "Rafael Inclan, as in Cuba's VP before, Fidel?" Carlos asked. "Are fourteen thousand Pedro Pan kids as smart as you?" Mario gutted Carlos with the football. "It doesn't matter who they were. Right now, they are stuck here, just like us." "Yeah, but they have a driver," Carlos said. Mom sent me to get Sheila. "You guys are weird," Sheila said.

The next day after school the limo showed up, Tony and "Fritos" (as we had begun to call Alfredo) jumped out of the car and walked toward my house. Tony ambushed Mario with a shove and pointed at me.

"Now's your chance to tell her you're jealous," Tony said. "I'm not jealous."

"Then ask her out, you know you want to. And remember, American girls aren't chaperoned like the Cubans."

Lourdes did not say a word, she just turned and walked home.

"Veronica, Mario has something to ask you," Sheila said. "No, she'd never bite," Mario said.

Just then Dad turned onto our street and tooted his horn. Sheila and I ran to see him.

Over dinner that night, Sheila proclaimed that big news on the street was that I had a boyfriend. Of course, I denied it, but Mom had neglected to tell Dad about my tutoring Antonio and Fritos, so he was more than interested to know what was going on with these boys in a limo.

I got a break when the news came on TV with a clip of President Kennedy talking about civil rights.

*We cannot say that your children cannot have the right to develop their talent, whatever it may be, due simply to the color of their skin.*

It did not matter after that anyway, because a few days later Antonio kissed me for real. I was shocked. My eyes kept blinking in astonishment. My first kiss was from the grandson of an ousted foreign dignitary. Not bad for a pigeon-toed, white-bread tomboy from South Florida.

Of course, Dad thought it was bad and put a stop to it. That was when I really noticed that it bothered Lourdes.

We were washing Mom's car to earn money, and Sheila chirped, "Dad said Veronica can't be kissing Antonio anymore."

I turned the hose on her. "Thanks to you."

Lourdes laughed a little too hard. Sheila thought she was laughing at her, but I knew that the way she looked at me that it was for a different reason. It did not matter because her and Sheila went at it just the same.

Sheila threw a sponge at her and got in her face about Cuba.

"Cuba got flattened by Hurricane Flora, and Castro won't accept American help."

"So," Lourdes shot back, "everyone knows Castro is insane." She turned the hose on Sheila, and we all let off a mountain of stress attacking each other.

# CHAPTER 28

One afternoon after ninth-grade exams, I decided to go into our backyard above-ground pool. It was fifty-five inches deep and twelve feet wide. It was plastic with a metal structural border and even had a filter. A ladder was needed to get in the pool, so we had one of those, too. I climbed the ladder and submerged instantly. I swam around the pool in my blue-and-white checked bikini with daisies embroidered on the waistband. The water felt so good that I turned over on my back to relax, and right in front of my face looking down at me was Brett. He was shocked, and I screamed. He scrambled back down the tree as my dad came out the back door. Let me tell you, my dad responded very quickly: the speed of his slide down the tree was just micro seconds I was so innocent back then and did not realize that I was about to find my first true love.

I got over Antonio and started hanging out with the white boy, Brett. He loved football, so he and Mario were always in some sort of sweaty competition. The only difference at that time was that Brett played for the Coral Gables Youth Center and played like a professional even at Kinloch Junior High.

Lourdes and I were still friends, but things were not the same for whatever reason.

With my neighborhood responsibilities shifting, I looked for new things to have in common with Dad. I liked to read the paper over his shoulder and try to make sense of the television news. One day, President Kennedy was coming back to give a speech at the Fontainebleau Hotel in Miami Beach. I needed to figure out how I could talk Dad into taking me, thinking he would jump at the chance. I made sure not to disturb his paper, so I waited until he was tinkering with his truck. "Not this time," he said. I was stunned at first that he knew I was going to say, but when it wore off, I resorted to be a whiny kid fighting for what I wanted. "Please, it's the president," I said. "It's a school night, and the city is just too heated right now," was Dad's reasoning.

I turned into the garage and saw my dusty bike with a flat tire, and I shoved it into the corner. "Roni," even though you are in junior high school, you are not an adult, and you cannot go to the president's speech. It is Miami, it will always be heated.

"I've never even been out of Florida, and now I can't go across the bridge to Miami Beach?"

"Next time."

I stomped off inside as a helicopter with the presidential seal whirred overhead.

The next day's paper had a story about Kennedy's visit and how he was supposed to ride through Miami in a convertible, but they canceled due to security concerns. So, I got over not being allowed to go to Miami Beach to see him. Dad was right.

A couple days later I was in the band room playing first chair clarinet to *West Side Story* when the intercom chime went off. The announcement that President Kennedy had been shot inside his motorcade rang out like a horrible attack on the US. One after another the band members sitting with their instruments shouted hysterical cries. A fire alarm bell rang, and we were all escorted outside as if it were a drill. But of course, it was not.

President Kennedy had left Miami for Tampa, and four days later, he arrived in Dallas. Apparently, his security detail thought Dallas was safer than Miami, and he rode with the top down.

President Kennedy was like a cool uncle to everyone in Miami. Everyone I knew anyway. However, some Cubans blamed him for the Bay of Pigs, which is why they thought Miami was a security risk.

How no one considered that Texas and guns go hand in hand is beyond me. I can tell you that day and the events leading up to it have been discussed and analyzed countless times, and every American citizen who gives a shit about their country knows every detail to a nightmarish end no matter how old they are. I am willing to bet people that were not even conceived of at the time know the history of the Kennedy assassination better than they know the history of the Revolutionary War that founded this country.

News flash, the *Miami Herald*'s front page, November 23, 1963, simply said: KENNEDY DEAD.

*On November 22, President Kennedy was shot while riding in an open-car motorcade through the streets of downtown Dallas. Less than an hour after the shooting, Lee Harvey Oswald killed a policeman who questioned him on the street. Thirty minutes after that, he was arrested in a movie theater by police. Oswald was formally arraigned on November 23 for the murders of President Kennedy and Officer J.D. Tippet.*

*On November 24, Oswald was brought to the basement of the Dallas police headquarters on his way to a more secure county jail. A crowd of police and press with live television cameras rolling gathered to witness his departure. As Oswald came into the room, Jack Ruby emerged from the crowd and fatally wounded him with a single shot from a concealed .38 revolver. Ruby, who was immediately detained, claimed that rage at Kennedy's murder was the motive for his action. Some called him a hero, but he was nonetheless charged with first-degree murder.*

Of course, the media is to blame, the grief only got worse with the president's funeral being televised. But before that, I was sitting quietly with Dad on the couch watching the news of Oswald being taken into custody. Sheila was half watching, but she was more interested in painting her nails with Mom's new Avon products.

Until the announcer on TV shouted, "Oswald's been shot."

I screamed, Sheila dropped the polish and screamed. Mom ran in and pulled us away from the TV while craning back to see it herself.

"This madness will never end," she said.

Not long after, the funeral was on all the channels. Mom smoked at least twenty cigarettes that day.

"Girls, why don't you go get some fresh air?" She pried us away from the set.

"You should, too," Dad said.

"What if we get shot?" Sheila asked.

Mom smashed out her cigarette from the long filter as the procession started and we all stood transfixed in front of the TV. When John Junior saluted his father's coffin, Mom broke down in tears.

"It's his birthday today," she said.

# CHAPTER 28

Not long after, once we had evolved beyond our state of shock, we all took a drive to the other coast of Florida to visit my Grandma in Saint Petersburg. I do not recall the reason for our visit, but it was a long enough drive, I remember feeling like the whole family was escaping. By the time we made it up and across the state, the late day sun had us in such a glare, Mom cautioned Dad not to drive into the bay. Then I saw this castle like structure, with copper spires that made the already bright sun do crazy things.

"Well that was fast," Dad said.

"We've been driving all day," Sheila said.

"I mean the sign. See that there: Tampa University is where the president was right before Dallas. They've already named the street after him."

"That's a school?" I asked.

"Gorgeous isn't it?" Mom said.

I do not recall an official family discussion or decision on the matter, but from that day onward, Dad saved every penny so I could go to that university.

Things in Miami eventually got back to a livable state of normal. But I do remember the neighborhood lost its sense of spunk for a long time; everyone was cynical and numb. I caught Mario on more than one occasion carving a dead chicken or lizard. Lourdes stayed in a lot more, and when I asked her about it, she said she was trying to teach her mom English. I offered to help, and she said "sure," but then she never followed up on it.

Then they started building a new high school that would ruin our friendship forever.

As if Miami was not already blatantly divided between Cuban and Caucasian, the new high school made sure the difference was clear. The boundary line for the two schools went straight through our little slice of Miami pie. Fifty-Seventh Avenue was the dividing line between attending old Miami High or new Coral Park High. Mom was tickled that we were on the Coral Park side. Here, I would be around fewer immigrants and blossoming inside a predominantly Jewish culture of upwardly mobile entrepreneurs from New York—like my mother's family. My sister Sheila and I had no designer clothes, but we learned quickly how to "imitate" and aspire to achieve. I remember being excited about meeting new people my age that were not Cuban. Not that I did not like Cubans. I adored them. And I was more than interested in being able to date Antonio now that I was in high school, but I was not one of them. I liked to blame Mario for me wanting to hang out with different people, his talks of Santeria and how chicken parts could bring a lifelong curse—or make someone fall in love, depending on how they were presented—got kind of gross after a while. But honestly, I did not think it was a big deal. It was just natural for kids to flock to the new and cool, same as it is today. Silly me.

Mom said I could have some kids from the neighborhood over for my birthday, which fell right at the start of the school year. It was fun to have our kitchen crowded with friends again. Dad carved a roast beef while Mom brought a cake to the table with fifteen candles blazing. Everyone sang, and I huffed and puffed my best to blow the candles out.

"What did you wish for?" Sheila asked.

Mom handed me a big gift—clearly a department store garment box.

"How about a new smashing outfit for Coral Park High? Jeez, I'm so glad we eked in over the boundary to go to a brand-new high school," she said.

Mom was so caught up in the moment she did not take time to read the room like she normally did. But I knew this was not something to talk about—not if I wanted to have a good birthday, anyway. I immediately saw Lourdes's jaw tighten.

"I'll open this later, when I can try it on," I said.

"Don't be silly, show your friends what you got," Mom said.

I pulled the nice outfit out of the box, careful not to bring up Coral Park again, but it was too late.

Lourdes's nostrils flared. "I knew you hated chaperoning us to school. Your Papa probably had Coral Park built for you, your perfectly square, white bread and white skin, white hair, now you can learn in white walls ... we made you suffer so much."

Lourdes ran through the crowded kitchen and out the door.

"Poor thing doesn't realize, no matter what high school you go to, the experience is torture." Mom proceeded to cut the cake and keep the rest of her guests satisfied.

As usual, Mom was right. Of everything I would go on to experience, high school was by far the worst. Of all the memories and milestones I am recalling, this part I could leave out and not blink. I honestly do not think anything in high school prepared, fulfilled, or put in perspective any part of life for me. Oh, I tried. Do not think for a second I did not go in gung-ho thinking I could run the place like I did our little grade school. I took up clarinet the first semester, and Sheila became a majorette, so we were both involved in school activities.

A new family moved into our neighborhood. This was the first white family to move in since all the refugees came in years before. They had a son, a year older than me. And because they were above Fifty-Seventh Avenue, he went to Coral Park with Sheila and me. Brett tried on many occasions to strike up a game with Mario. But Mario and some of the Miami High Cubans toughened considerably and quickly. I kept my mouth shut and focused on my clarinet, but it was clear that all the trust and assistance I gave them meant nothing now. Carlos had an uncle that made it to Chicago, so he went to stay there. I felt bad for Mrs. Achterkirch. She went back to being suspicious of everyone and a little less ornery than she had been.

I was anxious to date Antonio again, and by the time Sheila got to Coral Park, she was gaga for his brother. The government gave the families who lost men in the Bay of Pigs compensation funds, so Lourdes had money to hold her Quinceañera. If you are familiar with sweet sixteen bashes, this is the Latino version that happens at fifteen. When Lourdes and I were still friends I learned that this event is the most critically important for a young Latino lady. Even more important than a wedding to many, this is the moment a girl becomes a woman (despite what your body's hormonal status is). This is like an offering to the cosmos for a Latino female.

"Because it is the go ahead for a girl to be independent until she marries, and her life becomes dedicated to her husband and then children," Lourdes said to me when we were comparing America to Cuba and still on speaking terms.

"How long is your independence supposed to last?" I asked.

"At most four years, if we don't have someone to marry by nineteen or twenty, we are considered difficult."

So, it came to be that Lourdes somehow invited the hot Cuban brothers to her Quinceañera, and Sheila and I went as their dates. I never investigated it, but I assumed we were invited because the event was like one of our block parties we used to have, only this was a formal event. The whole neighborhood was there except for Brett and his family, and I figured that was because they did not understand the Latin American culture.

The celebration was in the Eden Roc hotel in Miami Beach. It was in a banquet room with matching tablecloths and balloons, a dance floor, and a band.

"I wonder what they do for a wedding?" Mom asked.

Lourdes did look like a bride: her gown made her look at least twenty, her hair was up, and she had a corsage. The bandleader called her out to the floor, and her grandma escorted her. She waved to the guests like a queen, which made us all laugh. I missed Lourdes's grandma almost more than I missed her. Lourdes replaced her flat shoes with fancy heels and led the first dance. Given that everyone lost their fathers and male figures in the Bay of Pigs, they had to improvise, and the bandleader told Lourdes to pick a dance partner. We all lined the dance floor. Lourdes walked the perimeter, beaming. She stopped in front of Antonio and me, and I swear to this day, she looked down on me and smirked. I did not see the exact order or exchange of events, but next thing I knew, she was dancing with my date.

Later, Lourdes came up to me. I thought she was going to apologize or maybe say hello, so when she hesitated, I jumped in.

"You look fantastic," I said.

"I'm surprised you came, you didn't have to," she said. "I figured with the Camarioca you'd be busy with new worms to raise." Lourdes turned and walked off before I even processed what she said.

Mrs. Achterkirch calmed me down. "Forget it," she said. "How many more Cubans can be coming?"

It was not until the next day when I could hijack one of Dad's papers that I learned what the Camarioca was. It was Castro's first boatlift to dump Cubans he did not want into Miami. It really did not register that this was a big deal. To me it seemed like they were already coming at a steady pace.

On September 25, 1965, President Fidel Castro of Cuba made a surprise announcement that Cubans with relatives in the United States would be permitted to leave the island if their relatives asked for them. Men of military age—fourteen to twenty-seven—were not permitted to leave. Castro's announcement forced the United States to define its immigration policy toward Cuba and resulted in a doubling of the number of Cuban refugees in the United States from 211,000 to 411,000.

Not long after Lourdes's so-called ceremony, Antonio asked me to the movies. In the mid-1960s we still had the newsreel promos before films, and when this one came on it was about President Johnson's freedom flights coming out of Cuba.

"Our neighborhood is full," I said. I meant it as a joke, but I guess it offended Antonio, so we did not date anymore after that. It was my first heartbreak, and like most, I did not know why it happened.

# CHAPTER 29

In her teens Sheila was selected to ride on the Queen's float in the Orange Bowl New Year's Eve parade. This debut was her opportunity to work in the fashion industry. She really became a shining star. She was a very pretty girl and was interested in fashion and makeup. Mom and Dad decided to send her to the Barbizon Fashion Institute to develop her natural skills. Sheila was so poised, walking her first runway like a star.

I, on the other hand, was going through a tough transition from the neighborhood kid responsible for everyone to a meek teenager sucking on her clarinet while trying to keep her pigeon toes pointed straight. I did get to join the marching band and marched in the Coral Park half-time shows. It was great to play in the stands at football games.

The battle of the Rams would go down as the thing I remember most about high school, and it was my first concrete clue that I needed to escape Miami. It was a fall Friday, which in Miami means more heat than anything else. Any student who was connected to band or football got to wear Coral Park Rams uniforms to school for the pep rally. By then, I was having fun dating a football player. Brett had become quite popular as a star player, which enabled me to teeter on cool once again, only this time I got to go along for the ride instead of being responsible for steering the ship.

The Coral Park Rams had an away game against Mays High in South Miami. Mays had an impressive football team that was all black. This was before segregation, so it was not that it was something to be feared, it was just a given. I was excited for the game, maybe it was my democratic upbringing, or maybe it was my work with the refugees at a young age, but the idea of going to a black school to play felt more like a perk than anything else. I suppose that is what Captain America and a president can instill in a person.

I can still picture our buses painted with Go Rams and our bouncy ride out to the middle of flat swamps that had us laughing and rolling out of our seats.

Once we got there, we hung out on the bus to prep our instruments and such until the teams were set, so we missed the beginning of the game. By the time we got to go to the field, it was dark, and the home team was losing. So, when they announced us, we were booed. I had my head down to play the clarinet and was in the rear of the marching formation, so I did not see, and was not looking, at what happened. All I know was that halfway into our first song, the entire band turned around in an unorganized heap and started running toward the buses we had just left.

We all clamored inside, dodging rocks and angry Mays students and fans. There were so many that they rocked the bus, and this time bouncing around and out of our seats was the single, most, scariest moment I had faced so far (and would be for years to come). I remember screaming and locking eyes with one of the attackers; I tried to reason with him through the small bus window. When that did not work, I begged him to stop. I saw a fear in his eyes that I am sure he saw in mine. I turned away and just sat on the bus seat and held on until police came, because at that moment I realized what it felt like to be transported somewhere you didn't belong and be expected to fit in without any problems.

It turns out, the whole country freaked out that night. Martin Luther King Jr., an American clergyman and civil rights leader, was fatally shot at the Lorraine Motel in Memphis, Tennessee. He was a prominent leader of the civil rights movement and a Nobel Peace Prize Laureate who was known for his use of nonviolence and civil disobedience.

Here I had spent my formative years shepherding and coddling Cuban immigrants when American blacks were experiencing some of the worst racism known to humankind. My mom I had been having premonitions indicating that I would have a chance to work in black communities in some way. I had no idea how I could help, but I was so happy to envision the possibility. But for now, I just left that open until I could see God's plan come to fruition. I was ready to get out of Miami, and my parents were all for me going away to college. I kept my nose in the books and my mouth to the clarinet while quietly dating Brett until we could get to Tampa University. Brett was going there, too. I liked to think it was because of me, but it turns out they had a good football program, and he received a full scholarship to attend. The place looked like the Taj Mahal, and we built it up in our minds that college would be like a four-year resort pass.

By the time I graduated I was chomping at the bit to be free. I knew I would be in Tampa in the fall, and in my mind, I had already expanded well beyond the confines of what I still considered my small beach town of Miami. So why not leave sooner? Mind you, it was the summer of 1969, and I was hanging out with a lot of spoiled rich kids in Miami even though I was neither of those things. But it is a nice feeling for a teenage girl to have connections. A girl named Janet and I had become friends in my senior year. She was from New York and was going back home for the summer. She had three tickets to a concert in Bethel, New York, called "Woodstock" and asked if I wanted to go. I told her I would tell my parents that I was spending the weekend in NYC with her, and I would drive since she had the tickets.

I drove my 1969 Hemi Roadrunner with a manual transmission to Bethel with two girlfriends, Janet, and Patti. Yes, it was a hot rod, and that is how I rolled. Had to fill up with high-test gas before we hit the road. Coincidentally, we found the flyer at the Pure Station on Flagler

Street. It announced the concert at a farm, so it seemed like a sign from the universe that we had to go. Three seventeen-year-old girls from la-la land Miami, took off for our first adventure without our parents.

We arrived in Bethel at around 4 p.m. on August 15. We could hear the music from our parking place two miles away. By late afternoon, none of the first four acts scheduled to lead off the festival had managed to make it to the site. Richie Havens, originally fifth on the bill, was ready and opened the festival. He took the stage at 5:07 p.m. and played to repeated standing ovations for almost three hours. Richie was followed (in order) by Sweetwater, The Incredible String Band, Bert Sommer, Tim Hardin, Ravi Shankar, Melanie, and Arlo Guthrie.

I was exhausted by midnight from the long drive and the pot fumes. A haze formed and it was not purple, it was gray and dingy like a fog in a Victorian murder mystery. It started raining again, smack in the middle of Shankar's set. I never heard of Shankar, but I was impressed by his pluckiness in braving the elements despite the rain. Eventually he had to stop after five songs. Rain would continue to fall heavily throughout the event, creating huge mud pits interrupting or delaying several performances. Joan Baez, my idol. Her contemporary folk music protested social injustice, and as a 1969 hippy it blew me away! She took the stage at about 1:00 a.m. to close the first day's performances. Throughout the night, the flow of people into Yasgur's Farm continued nonstop. Every time someone stepped over me lying on my ragged car towel, I woke up with a jolt.

A medical tent was set up to treat bare feet cut by broken glass and metal can lids that littered the site, bad acid trips, and retinas burned when stoners lied down while staring directly at the sun. A young man, asleep in a trash-strewn field, hidden under his sleeping bag for protection from the rain, died when a tractor hauling away sewage from the portable toilets accidently ran over him. Shit, what a way to die.

In nearby Bethel, volunteers began making thousands of sandwiches that would be sent by helicopter to the site to feed the hungry masses. The Town Justice held court in his living room to deal with nearly two hundred drug-related cases.

The second day's festival performances, originally scheduled to start in the evening, began shortly after noon so that the crowd did not become restless and unruly. Artists were asked to lengthen their sets to keep the peace. Quill, Keef Hartley Band, "Country Joe" McDonald, John Sebastian, Santana, Canned Heat, Mountain, Grateful Dead, Creedence Clearwater Revival, Janis Joplin, Sly and the Family Stone, The Who, and Jefferson Airplane all played on the second day. Technical problems prevented Quill's performance from being included in Woodstock (the movie) causing Atlantic Records to drop them. Electrical problems and ankle-deep water on stage literally shocked the hell out of the Grateful Dead. Sparks radiated as they were electrocuted when they touched their microphones and electric guitar strings. All were grateful they were not dead. Throughout the day, rain and technical delays wreaked havoc with the festival schedule. The Who finished their set as the sun rose on Sunday morning, and it was nearly 8:00 a.m. Sunday when Saturday night's headline act, Jefferson Airplane, finally started playing. Scheduled Saturday night performances did not end until mid-morning Sunday, so there was a little gap between Jefferson Airplane and Joe Cocker, who took the stage at 2:00 p.m. with storm clouds looming.

I could not find Janet or Patti. I was hoping they did not succumb to the to the urging of drug dealers wanting sex. Yes, I was a goody two-shoes. This dirty disgusting place did not feel right to a strong Virgo girl. I could not wait to hear more music, which was the one saving grace. I prayed for rain just to feel a little clean again. *Damn, I should have brought soap.* I kept saying to myself, *Veronica, you will live through this to brag to your friends and strangers about it.* I was not the only one feeling out of place. I watched the firefighters trudge through the mud all sweaty and exhausted with anguished faces that I never forgot.

The third day after Joe Cocker's set, there was a two-hour thunderstorm delay, after which the day's lineup continued at around 6:00 p.m. with Country Joe and the Fish, Ten Years After, The Band, Johnny Winter, Crosby, Stills, Nash, and Young, Paul Butterfield Blues Band, Sha-Na-Na, and Jimi Hendrix. I was wandering around aimlessly when a good-looking firefighter walked up to me. He asked me why I was not galivanting around with the others. As a seventeen-year-old daddy's girl, I ran and jumped on him, wrapping my legs around him. He was taken aback literally. He was swaying a little. We were face to face, eyes to eyes. It was very weird. He just stood there holding me, and I clung on for dear life. Finally, it was evident that he was working and should not be carrying a blonde teenager around, so he let me down. He saw the fright in my face. He told me that he would be assigned to the concert for the duration and that he would be walking around near the telephone stands if I needed him. His name was Lt. Bradshaw. I was so relieved that I jumped up and kissed him on the cheek. When I say up, he was probably at least six-feet-four.

# CHAPTER 30

Neil Young played for the first time with Crosby, Stills and Nash, performing only two songs in the band's acoustic set and refused to be filmed during their electric set, complaining that the cameras were too distracting. I was so in awe of their pure love of music as they brushed off publicity. It was so humid that Ten Years After could not keep their guitar strings in tune. Sadly, because of technical problems, only the band's last song was filmed.

Two more deaths, both from drug overdoses, occurred Saturday. There were four births. Three babies were born in a temporary clinic that had been set up by an area hospital in a school just off the festival grounds. The fourth baby was born at a motel in nearby Bethel. It was the first place the new daddy could find when his wife went into labor.

What had been scheduled as a three-day (Friday to Sunday, August 15 to 17) festival continued well into the morning of Monday, August 18, due to the numerous rain delays and technical glitches. A mass exodus began when a thunderstorm delayed the proceedings (yet again) at about 5:00 p.m. on Sunday. An estimated thirty-five thousand attendees stayed through to the end of the final performance, which began at 9:00 a.m. Monday.

As the festival ended, estimates of the number of people who attended varied widely. The state police estimate was 450,000, however I think it rounded to half a million. A newspaper editor on the scene claimed the total was probably closer to 150,000, but a Bethel historian says it was closer to 700,000. Due to the lack of an adequate ticket selling and collecting system, we will never know for sure. When they added it all up, festival organizers figure they were $1.3 million in debt, with expenses more than 300 percent over budget and most attendees getting in without having paid for a ticket. Since I arrived on Friday, the first day, I paid for three days, and it cost me $35. More than five thousand people required medical treatment during the festival. Of that total, about eight hundred involved drug use. There were eight reported miscarriages. It cost $100,000 and several days to clean up the site. Workers bulldozed tons of trash and debris into a pit and burned it.

I am still haunted by so much sex, drugs, and rock and roll. Blankets in the mud, naked bodies sprawled out exhausted from multiple orgasms and strung out on whatever psychedelics they consumed. I knew to save my 17-year-old virginity I had to take on a kick-ass biker chick persona. It worked, and I kept referring to "Lizard, my old man" steering the badly demented, scary, sexually driven hippy boys away. So, I survived the new sexual revolution for the time being, anyway.

I never saw Lt. Bradshaw again, but I always remember his kindness. In a small way, he was *my hero*. The summer of 1969 opened my innocent eyes to dirty sex and mayhem. I should not have gone to Woodstock. I was a virgin and waiting to be married to Brett. What had I gotten myself into by following instead of my usual take-charge attitude? All it did for me is open my eyes to the future of college in the 70's, as the Viet Nam killing fields evolved into sights of helicopters flying out with the wounded on television.

I looked around for Janet, and she was nowhere to be seen. Thank God I spelled out on an old piece of newspaper, the time and location of our meeting place. Janet and Patti finally showed up and we began our two-mile walk back down the road to find the Roadrunner.

In retrospect, I had no idea what would happen as I walked through the farm fields trying to find a spot to settle with my towel. I was a jock's girlfriend, not a hippy, at least not yet anyway. I was mesmerized by the colorful flowing dresses, leather fringed vests, head, and armbands of leather. I did have the appropriate long, straight blonde hair, and my jeans were not worn or torn. My top was a simple T-shirt from Sears. As time went on, the mud and rain created a tie-dye-like swirl on my clothes which buried the Ivy League girl look.

The epic event would later be known simply as "Woodstock", synonymous with the counterculture movement of the 1960s. Woodstock was a success, but the massive concert did not come off without a hitch: last-minute venue changes, bad weather, and the hordes of attendees caused major headaches. Still, despite (or perhaps because of) a lot of sex, drugs, rock 'n' roll and rain, Woodstock was a peaceful celebration and earned its hallowed place in pop culture history. I was thankful for the experience but even more "grateful" that I was not dead.

# CHAPTER 31

I started college in August of 69 and turned 18 that September 5th. I celebrated at my first frat party, as they circled me dancing to the Beatle's song, *today is your Birthday, your gonna have a good time!* That alone scared me and stimulated me at the same time. It was a new world with new friends and lots to look forward to.

As the 70's rolled in, this fully immersed hippy wore bright striped hip-hugging bell bottoms called *landlubbers*. I kept my hair long with a black leather silver studded hand band with matching arm bands. My skirts were way too short, and I wore *monster* shoes, which were huge clunky leather-clog-looking things with huge metal buckles. I fell often on the red brick roads to class at the University of Tampa. Now that I look back, they looked pilgrim like and emphasized my big, muscular thighs. Not a good look for a dainty girl. Oh well, I was in total fashion even if the hippy movement was waning in 1969. My mom was very thankful for the beginning a new era.

Patti, one of the girls I went to Woodstock with, was my new best friend and somehow her mom and mine were fine with whatever we did because they were both New Yorkers trying to make sense of life in Florida—if they only knew how we chose to do so. Come to think of it, Mom must have known but chose to ignore our phase of rebellion. Patti, ended up going to college in Tampa with me. Another girl that she knew from Southampton, became our roommate. I thoroughly enjoyed this free spirit life but kept a quiet watch on how Dad's money was spent. Even though I was not living at home, the time with these upper-crust girls from New York brought me closer to Mom. For the first time, I realized not only what she gave up for love, but the source of her outspoken frustrations about life in Florida. I hoped there was way more out there than gators, beaches, and palm trees, and I was happy to make this connection with her perspective. Because until now, my formative years were all about behaving in a way that warranted Dad's approval, not because he demanded it, but because I idolized him.

There was still a lot of racial tension. If anything, being outside of Miami, made me see just how racially twisted the rest of the country was. Our school hosted a black college for a football game. Unlike at high school, this had never been done before, and we were all in the spotlight. The Tampa Spartans vs. the Florida A&M Rattlers game had a lot of national publicity, simply because it was the first interracial college football game. It brought back memories of that away game in high school—especially with Brett playing. I did not like being placed in a position where I had to feel concerned. "Why can't we just play"? Why do they have to harp on the color of the athletes' skin?" I asked. Brett, who was considered the star of the team, agreed. "I just want to play, too, babe."

The game made me uncomfortable, and once we got in the stands the place was clearly divided between black and white. It was as if half of the stadium was in shadow. The girls and I made partied as always, and soon it was just like any other game. Only this one was close, very close. A&M beat us, but to me I was so pumped up with how close the game was, it was all I wanted to talk about with Brett afterward. He was so depressed about losing. We broke up soon after that game. I guess the pressure of the real world was too much for two strong personalities. Brett transferred to FSU on another full scholarship. Little did I know that he would go on to play with the Green Bay Packers, where (at the time) a predominantly white population wore cheese on their heads to show their support. What the heck?

I am so proud of my university. The minute I saw it from the expressway going to visit my grandma Sally in St. Petersburg in 1967, I knew I had to attend. The beauty of the Victorian/Moorish architecture was astonishing. I was only 15 when I first saw it, and if I had recognized my love of buildings, I would have studied to be an architect. However, I would not have been able to get that degree at U of T, it was a liberal arts school.

The building called Plant Hall is the main academic and administrative building of the university: it already had an extraordinary history. Formerly the Tampa Bay

Hotel, the building remains a symbol of the city and its history. Local historians credit its builder, railroad, and shipping magnate Henry B. Plant, with the transformation of Tampa from a sleepy fishing village to what would become a vibrant twenty-first-century city. Built between 1888 and 1891, the hotel was designed to surpass all other grand winter resorts. At a cost of $3 million, the 511-room giant rose to a flamboyant height of five stories, surrounded by ornate Victorian gingerbread and topped by Moorish minarets, domes, and cupolas. The rooms that once hosted Teddy Roosevelt, the Queen of England, Booker T. Washington, Stephen Crane, and Babe Ruth (who signed his first baseball contract in the hotel's grand dining room) are now classrooms, laboratories, and administrative offices: the heart of The University of Tampa and a landscape for state-of-the-art student learning environments. Today, the University of Tampa serves more than 9,304 undergraduate and graduate students, and Plant Hall remains the foundation of a 110-acre, 60-building campus that successfully blends the historic with the modern. Known for academic excellence, personal attention and real-world experience in its undergraduate and graduate programs, University of Tampa students come from 50 states and 132 countries. Presently, there are more than 200 programs of study, including 16 master's degree programs, one doctorate and numerous study abroad opportunities. From its humble beginnings in Plant Hall, UT boasts a $300 million annual revenue and a $1 billion estimated annual economic impact.

By the time I graduated college in 1973, I figured I would go on to be a teacher since my BS degree is in Education. However, I was not sure what level I wanted to teach. I had gotten a taste of the wild-life and did not think I had what it took to mold young minds. Honestly, I had no idea what I was going to do with my life. And when faced with the real world, I questioned my choice of major. From the time I was little, I thought being a teacher would be a great job. It is one of the reasons I loved helping the immigrant children when they came to our neighborhood. I loved the responsibility of it and the reward when they understood something I explained. I was looking forward to going back to where it all started and figuring it out.

My graduation from the University of Tampa in 1973 was so elegant. It was held in Walker Hall a historical building behind Smiley Hall, my dorm. Our professors were former professors from major universities across the country. The university president lured them to University of Tampa. The Florida climate was their motivation to go back to work.

Mom, Dad, and Sheila all attended my graduation. The 4-hour trip back home to Miami, was full of a lot of talk about Nixon and how many Cubans were now in Miami. I guess my parents were using the time to educate me on the world away from academia.

Nixon began his presidency at noon EST on January 20, 1969, when he was inaugurated as the 37th president of the United States. Sadly, his reign ended on August 9, 1974, when he resigned in the face of almost certain impeachment, and removal from office, the only US president ever to do so.

The freedom flights were still going on adding 270,000 Cubans, since I had received my degree in education. I realized how much I missed tagging along with all of Dad's thoughts about government and civic duty; I really fed off the way his mind worked. I loved everything about that ride until we got close to home.

"What happened to the Winn Dixie?" I asked.

"It's a Sedano's," Mom said. "You can't get a decent coke and chips, but you can get tortillas and guava juice." Graffiti was sprayed across barbershops and Woolworths had bums begging out front. Interesting enough that the bums were both white and black homeless folks. The jobs they had were taken by new people happy to take lower salaries. Every street we turned down on the way home showed signs of wear and new life: overpopulation with no regulation.

If you have never seen a Florida bungalow, especially one built in the late 1940s, early 1950s, they are essentially cinderblock "Monopoly" houses sealed with decades of pastel paint. There are no basements, only exterior crawl spaces that without mesh or lattice all sorts of critters move in. The bungalows are small, with beautiful roofs built of white concrete S-shaped tiles called "Spanish tile" but made in Cuba before the revolution. The walls were CBS block and stucco, sturdy enough to withstand a hurricane, if the roof stayed on. At the time these were built, strong white concrete shingle roofs came with the budget—nothing truly durable like the fancy terra cotta of the Coral Gables homes. The only exterior accessories they came with were colorfully striped aluminum shutters that could be pulled down and bolted to the cinder block exteriors when a storm was brewing. If you have never had to use hose or sprinkler water in Florida, you would think there were rotten eggs in the pipes when you turned them on. The water we used outside is heavy with sulfur, which smells rotten and stains, sidewalks, and pastel paints.

Upon entering our neighborhood after being away for so long, I saw the water stains and weathered roofs. Lattice rots after one year; imagine it after twenty. There were no lattice sheets made of PVC like today. Every house in our community needed fresh paint, modern roofing, and other new materials to keep critters out.

"It's not the Taj Mahal, is it?" Mom said.

I shook it off, ashamed that she said aloud what I was thinking. "It's home," I said. "I'm happy to help you paint." I looked to Dad to see if he would bite at the invitation.

"Let's get you settled," he said. "Making good use of that degree we invested in is job one."

Then I saw Mrs. Achterkirch's house. There was a hot rod parked in the driveway. Metallic orange, with big glossy black tires, the rear tires were twice the size of the front. I cracked up.

"Mrs. A" traveling in style." I said.

Nobody responded.

"Is she okay? I mean I never thought about it, but I figured you'd say something if she died or moved."

"I haven't seen her for a while," Mom said. "She must have company."

And just like that, I was made to recognize the fact that I was not coming home to a community; I was coming home to the family roof over my head. Looking back, I imagine that is what most Americans were going through. There is a reason that *Happy Days* and the *Andy Griffith Show* were set in the fifties in a small town. The idyllic American life was all but gone by the seventies, although I do wonder what type of neighborhood Ron Howard raised his children in, considering the picture he painted for the world. I wonder if he feels a responsibility for the way other countries think about the American way of life.

Anyway, I spent the first couple of days feeling nostalgic and going through the things in my room. But I quickly grew stir crazy and decided to walk the old stomping grounds. I looked to Lourdes's house, it was quiet and in need of some TLC, too. I wondered how her grandma was doing, more than I did Lourdes, anyway. Thinking about Lourdes made me sad; I never really understood why we stopped being friends. In my mind it seemed as if she blamed me not only for going to Coral Park High but also for not being Cuban. As I looked at her house, I daydreamed about all of the times in my childhood that I could have been doing other things instead of hanging out with her and the other Cubans who needed assistance: things like going to the beach or riding my bike. I realized I was not sad for the time lost, because I felt like the responsibility I was given opened me to a whole other world that I would have never known. I was sad for the friendship that dissolved almost as quickly as it formed. Even though I was just out of college, I knew then what so many adults learn later on in life: how fleeting even the best friendships are and how rare it is to find someone who shares enough of the same perspective as you to make it comfortable to hang together. I contemplated knocking on her door and apologizing (even though I do not think I did anything wrong). I realized that I had found a common perspective with someone from another country, someone who barely spoke English, and that it was even rarer than most friendships that fade away.

"Veronica?"

A male voice snapped me out of my daydream. I turned to see the owner of the hot rod in Mrs. Achterkirch's driveway.

"Carlos?"

We ran to each other and hugged tightly.

"Wow, you look great," he said.

"So, do you!"

We both asked, "Are you visiting?" in unison, and it dawned on me that I had found the common perspective I was yearning for.

Carlos had been living in Chicago with his uncle, and when he became old enough, he said he wanted to return to Miami. He was still holding out hope that his parents would make it out of Cuba on one of the freedom flights. They had come close a couple of times but got sent to the back of the line for ridiculous reasons, usually because someone more important or with more money came along and took their spots.

"Plus, Chicago is so cold, I will never get used to ice cold wind blowing through my head and up my pant legs—do you know how that can affect a guy coming of age?"

That was Carlos, he never minced words or hesitated to paint a funny visual to make a point.

Mrs. A. was happy for the company and had Carlos staying there in exchange for work on her house. As a result, her house looked the best on the street, even better than ours, which I am sure pushed Dad's buttons.

Carlos convinced me to go downtown with him for some drinks. Not that it took a lot of convincing for a girl, home from college with no car, to go out for some fun. Little did he know I had a 1969 red 289 Mustang with silver baby-moon hubcaps, and I did not tell him. It was fun to be driven around for a while. This is when I got a real dose of how much Miami had changed. When I left for college, my introduction to partying was at Woodstock. While I fully get the idea that this was more like a spiritual awakening into the world of mind-altering substances, it was like an escalator that carried me right over the phase of the naïve high schooler sneaking into bars. So, I did not have a lot of firsthand experience with all that Miami had become, but boy was I about to make up for lost time.

We met up with a friend of his who I met when we were in grade school. Fernando Valdes came over on the Pedro Pan flight with Carlos. He was supposed to be in fifth grade, but a week later he was sent back to third grade because of his English.

"Oh my, God. You're the girl Carlos said would tutor me, but I didn't know what *tutor* meant," Fernando said.

"And you're the boy who came to Miami with a bottle of rum to trade for food," I said.

"Some things never change," Carlos joked.

"When Carlos he skipped town, I was lost. I was thirteen by the time I got out of grade school!"

We were at Big Daddy's, the original. In the next five years there would be about twenty Big Daddy's bars across Florida. They were the first bars serving food that were open year-round in south Florida's tourist area of Downtown Miami. By 1980, they all had a rep and so did their owner. But they eventually closed and became the burger/bar chain called Flannigan's, that are still all over Florida. Fernando was in "Big Daddy's" pocket; he was selling used Corvettes, which in the seventies were big business.

I got home late that night. Mom and Dad did not say anything; they knew I was with Carlos. The next night, Fernando came to pick me up in a candy-apple red Corvette, I could feel Mom and Dad peeking out from the blinds like Gladys Kravitz from *Bewitched*, but they did not say a word.

# CHAPTER 32

Fernando and I started seeing each other every night. I was easily in love, and he was a great excuse for me not to ease into the world of adult responsibility too soon. It was the birth of disco, and I had a hot Latino with a hot car. At first, I felt like I had earned the right to be a little irresponsible, considering the way I had lived the first part of my life. As weeks went on, I could feel Mom's arched eyebrows, and every time Dad rattled his paper, I felt like it was a call that I was ignoring.

"School is starting soon," Mom said. "Any teaching interviews lined up?"

My head was numb from the night before and I could not think fast enough, so I just said, "Yeah, tomorrow," and went back to my room.

"Do you want to remind her the of the point of an expensive college education?" Mom asked Dad.

"She knows." I heard him say.

That day I got dolled up and went looking for a job. Fernando knew a lot of businessmen downtown, so I started there. I still was not sure how to use my BS in Education degree, but I had a feeling being in a classroom was not the way to go. I went to an office and interviewed with a Cuban guy who had a hair perm and a healthy mustache. I could not stop staring at the hair that engulfed him, and he must have thought I was daft. The next day, he got me in front of a bank manager. That interview went well until I asked about how they deal with robberies.

Dad turned off the lawnmower when he saw Fernando drop me off.

"Any luck?"

In that split second, I wanted to run to him and hug him and never let go. I never dreamed I would not be able to walk into any place and ask, "When do I start?" It is not like I was on the verge of homelessness, but I was on the verge of uselessness. But if it had not been for Fernando, I would have been climbing the walls.

"Overqualified," I said.

"How can you be overqualified when you've got no experience?"

"I put too much emphasis on my community service and grades... I guess."

Dad put his arm around me and walked me to the door. I felt him watch Fernando drive off.

"I've missed our talks," he said.

"I'm not in the mood for a lecture."

"No one ever is." He stopped. It was the kind of stop that makes whoever is in its wake take notice and stop, too.

He pulled a slip of paper out of his wallet, unfolded it slowly, and handed it to me. "You can do what you want with this, I don't want to make you be anything you don't want to be," he said.

I could feel guilt coming from him, like he was handing me a draft notice. I was almost afraid that is what it was.

"I've had enough influence on your career choices, you have to decide for yourself—and I'll be okay with it," he said.

I read the paper, twice. I folded it in half and hugged him. Maybe I was hormonal, but I like to think that this was a bonding moment to make up for the years I was trying on Mom's shoes in high school, college, and beyond, and that would explain the stream of tears rolling down as I held him tight.

"I've missed your influence," I said. "Thank you. You've always known what was best for me."

Dad pulled away enough for me to see his surprise and delight.

The paper was a note to confirm a job interview with the city manager of Miami. They were looking for a director of their new childcare initiative in Miami's burgeoning ethnic areas.

"I didn't save every penny for you to work a dead-end job," he said. "Jack is an old friend, but he won't pull any punches if you don't make the cut. He is sharp as a tack and does not like to repeat himself. But underneath he's got a heart of gold."

"So, he's just like you."

"If that's the case, you'll have a long and successful career."

# CHAPTER 33

My interview with Jack Williams, the Miami city manager was a walk and talk, baptism by fire. Fernando had a meeting to get a lease for his exotic car lot, so he dropped me off at a daycare facility, not yet open, in Little Havana.

To say Fernando was driven is like saying Miami is hot, but his drive was all about helping his parents get back everything they lost under Castro. He found a direct route with his high-end cars. I suppose that is the difference between real drive and plain motivation: it is a Porsche compared to a Chevy. Both get you where you want to go, but one does it so much faster with a splashier entrance. That is what I loved about Fernando. he had all the looks of a Latino hustler. But he had the heart of a dedicated family man.

The daycare was due to open any day. Construction workers were hanging signs, while inspectors tested plumbing and outlets.

"This will be the first of three facilities to open this year, but we're already looking at plans for more to break ground," Jack said.

We were going over the outdoor area when a young Cuban woman with a baby tried to go inside.

"Come back next week, we should be open, and if not, there will be staff to help you at least." He leaned in and whispered to me, "If we're not open next week, I'll be dead."

I smiled to the woman, who looked strung out on something, and Jack and I continued the tour.

When we got back inside and he was showing me the office and the plans of operation, I looked up, sure that I heard someone.

"The person I need must be an educator but also someone who does not shy away from racial differences, poverty..."

Next thing I know a construction worker called out, "There's a baby in here."

Jack and I ran to find the baby the woman had when she was there, not two minutes before.

Jack ran after the woman, but she was nowhere to be found. The baby's wails echoed through the empty facility. I picked her up to calm her, and she puked all over my interview suit. That shut her up simply fine.

Jack came in and saw I took control. "Where was I? Oh yeah, so you have to be able to handle, uh—"

"Puke."

"Can you start tomorrow?"

I could have been a hooker at that point, and he would have hired me. But truth be known, it was a perfect job for someone with my life experience and education. In no time, I was unpacking supplies and hiring help. Within a week, Shenandoah Day Care Center opened in Little Havana. Within two months, similar centers were opened in Little Haiti, Moore Park on Thirty-sixth Street and Seventh Avenue and Edison in the northeast, near Edison High School.

Dad manned the grill for a celebration dinner. Any event that gave him an excuse to pull out his spatula was a good one. I ran up to Mrs. Achterkirch to invite her and Carlos to join us. But as soon as I stepped on the front sidewalk, I could see that was not going to happen. There was an ambulance in their driveway—no lights, no sirens. I ran as fast as I could. When I got there, I found Carlos at the front door as the EMTs lifted the gurney with Mrs. A on it. I could tell by his face that it was no use. Mrs. Achterkirch was dead. I just hugged him, and we both cried as they wheeled her away.

Fernando and I became a young power couple. His car business took off, and we spent our nights amid Miami's elaborate disco era. He had a loyal following of exotic car dealers. They traded, sold, and bought these things like kids do video games. One of his best customers gave him a flashy gold necklace with a medallion of a black tuna on it. It was gaudy, but we both seemed swept up in the flash and the cash of it all.

After buying and selling Corvettes from his front yard, Fernando opened Specialty Automobiles on Twenty-seventh Avenue, and money came rolling in. That is when he realized what the 18K gold black tuna necklace meant.

We hung out with the new faces of success in Miami. He bought a new "cigarette" speedboat that we were out on every weekend. It was the perfect escape from my day-to-day dealings with the children who needed way more than daycare to get a leg up. I had the benefit of understanding the Cuban culture, but I got that understanding from families that were fairly stable. In the Little Havana daycare, I had to quickly understand families like Olivia's, the little girl who was left there before the facility was even open. Her mom, who I came to know as Maria, fully believed that we were there to take care of her little girl on her terms, and she was not the only one. We had Santeria, Haitian Voodoo, and Espiritismo fanatics. I learned about Espiritismo the hard way. I had boxes of spare T-shirts and underpants ordered for the kids who came in filthy or without a change of clothes. But those who were deeply involved in this belief system are strictly forbidden to wear anything but white on certain days. I had a mother strip her child bare, happy to take him out naked rather than in clean clothes that were not white.

Since I am a very intense person and loved my children so much, I dove into research on the various cultural and spiritual beliefs of the parents of my children. Spiritism, known as Espiritismo in Spanish, is the religious belief in the power and ability of spirits to affect human life. This type of spiritualism is practiced by many Caribbean peoples, as well as citizens of Latin America.

The phenomenon and broad range of beliefs defined as "Espiritismo" originated with the ideas of Spiritism defined by Allen Kardek. His Spiritism would become popular in Latin America and influence existing religions as well as forming Africanized traditions of Espiritismo itself. It would become especially prominent in Cuba and Puerto Rico. Scientific White Table Espiritismo would develop from a loose understanding of Kardec's philosophy. During the ten years of war in Cuba, much of the population was in panic and grieving from the loss of loved ones. White Cubans were able to alleviate some of their emotional pain by turning to Espiritismo, which allowed them to commune with dead loved ones. White *espiritistas* would ask their Congolese slaves to guide them in Espiritismo de Cordon ceremonies. In the early 1800s Espiritismo would gain popularity in Puerto Rico because of the populace's rejection of Spanish hegemony and Spiritism's condemnation by the colonial Catholic Church. Originally brought to the country from Puerto Ricans studying in Europe the White Table Espiritismo practiced by the upper class would evolve into a more Creolized indigenous Espiritismo among the underclass. Researcher Marta Moreno Vega suggests Puerto Rican Espiritismo became popular as a way to mimic ancestor veneration in Kongo religion.

Espiritismo in Cuba would eventually mix with other local African elements and produce Espiritismo Cruzao, which would become popular in the early 1900s. By the time of the Cuban Revolution, *espiritista* practices were banned and pushed underground but still retain a presence in Cuban society to this day. Cuban Americans and Puerto Rican Americans residing in New York and New Jersey began to meld the beliefs of Santeria and Espiritismo, which became Santarismo. This cult like religion was first noticed by religious anthropologists in the 1960s.

My research helped me understand and accept the various religions. Thank God I had done my research before I was confronted with multiple divided palm fronds stuck into the ground in one single point right in from my Haitian childcare center called City of Miami Little River Day Care. Believe me I hung onto this palm frond explanation praying I was accepted. I read that Voodoo is hierarchical and includes a series of initiations.

# CHAPTER 34

Fernando's friend Joe was a high-rolling real estate agent in Miami. His wife, Sherri, worked at the Bank of America and was recently promoted to VP. So, to celebrate, all four of us flew to Escuintla, Guatemala, to stay on Fernando's uncle's sugar plantation. After the Bay of Pigs, his uncle married a Guatemalan woman and acquired her family's sugar plantation. It was a massive home, built of coquina which is a sedimentary rock which is composed of fragments of shells and mollusks. Being Cuban and a natural entrepreneur, he worked a deal with friends in Miami to sign a contract to supply sugar to the Bacardi Rum company headquartered in Miami.

"So that's why Bacardi is like money to you," I said.

"My family is close," Fernando said. "We look out for each other, if I have to sell a thousand Corvettes stocked with Bacardi to get my parents here, I will."

Fernando did not get I was making a joke, and he really did not want to think about those days when he was little and did not have much food after losing his estate in

Camaguey. Maybe that is why he enjoyed being so flashy now. Anyway, that was the last time I mentioned Bacardi. I do not even think I drank it after that weekend. A bottle of Bacardi and one bag of clothes were his sole possessions when he entered the United States. The bottle was sent with him to barter for food.

We got back to vacation mode and rode horses around the plantation where the workers walked around with machetes to slice through the cane at any given moment. We even rode up the mountain adjacent to the plantation. We had to hang on tight, hugging the horses' necks riding almost vertically *up, up, and away.*

The plantation workers were fascinated with my white-blonde hair hanging to my waist and called out, "Rubia!" I carried a machete on my horse and posed for them. That made their day.

Daily we climbed onto the conveyor belts, riding with the sugar cane to the liquidation process. It was extremely dangerous, but we were total risk takers, and it was fun to leap to safety right before the choppers went into action.

We all decided to rent a car to go see the Miss Universe Pageant in El Salvador. As always Fernando was thinking of his family, so we rented the exact same car as his uncle's, then Fernando and Joe proceeded to exchange new parts from the rental car and install them into his uncle's car. Then we left the rental car at the plantation.

On the drive to El Salvador, we were stopped at the border because Fernando was Cuban. El Salvadorans hate Cubans because much of the local land was bought up by Cubans after the revolution, much like it was in Miami. They finally let us go, and we made it to the beach. We stopped for huge, freshwater Rio oysters and ate them right out of the river. We left a huge pile of shells behind. I still have my photo album showing the garb we wore to blend into the native habitat. My hair was tightly pinned up under a ball cap.

At the river, I kind of heard Joe asking the locals about marijuana. He did not speak Spanish, so Fernando jumped in. I think we were in Guatemala for a drug deal, and to this day I have no idea what was actually happening.

We arrived in El Salvador just in time for an early dinner. We decided to eat before the pageant. The restaurant, like most in El Salvador, was in an open-air building. Picnic-type wooden tables and benches completed the junglelike décor. While we were eating, I let down my hair because the tight knot on top of my head started to hurt. Whoa, was that a mistake. Local men came out of nowhere and started hanging on the open roof rafters doing pull-ups and flexing their muscles. Fernando was enraged, so we left immediately, thus avoiding a full-on Cuban-Guatemalan conflict.

We ran to the car and jumped in. Fernando gunned it. Thank God it took off spraying pebbles and sand all over them. We kept going until we arrived where the Miss Universe 1975, was held.

The pageant was held on July 19, 1975 at the National Gymnasium in San Salvador, El Salvador. The Pageant was magnificent. The contestants were gorgeous dressed in their beautiful gowns, some in their native costumes. I was very amazed at the swimsuit competition. They had perfect bodies and were so graceful in their high heels. I thought to myself, *how brave they must be to walk almost naked across the stage.* The music was tantalizing, like a young girl's dream, my dream that would never happen. The final five contestants were from Finland, Haiti, USA, Philippines, and Sweden. They were a motley line of women. I was so impressed that the judges recognized the beauty in their diversity.

Anne Marie Pohtamo won the title for Finland, thus making her the second Finnish woman to win the Miss Universe crown after Armi Kuusela, who was the first Miss Universe winner, in 1952. The political backdrop to the 1975 Miss Universe pageant was not a happy one. I felt the invisible fog of tension flow throughout the building and kept glancing around. My mom's soothsayer vibes came all the from Miami in huge thrusts of fear.

As we walked out of the gym to get into the car, we heard gun shots. Crowds of people ran out of the gym screaming "comunistas" deluged with various expletive words in Spanish. We did not understand why they were rioting. Bottles were thrown cracking people in the head. Blood was spewing out all over the sidewalk. I just stood there and stared; I had never seen so much bloody fighting. Sounds of gun fire and bullets shooting passed causing me to fall to the ground thinking I was shot. I felt my whole body for entry wounds and could not find any. I flipped out as the terrifying screams pierced the air. I was pulled up by a strange looking man and shoved along through the crowd. The wonderfully enigmatic man abruptly, dropped me under a bush and kept running. I stayed low with my eyes closed praying every single second! I saw Sherri crawling low along the edge of the grass. I was afraid to call out to her, as I prayed, she would make it out alive. Suddenly, I saw Fernando and Joe running, yelling at us to *hurry and get in the car*. It seemed like déjà vu. We stood up and ran with all our might until we reached the car. It was a miracle that all four of us jumped into the car and screeched away, like a bat out of hell.

Stealthy thugs came out of nowhere chasing us through the woods in Jeeps. It seemed to me they were prepared for this—at least more than we were. It was dark as we swerved through the rain forest. Sounds of parrots and monkeys screeched at us. Sherri and I were freaking out, while ducking down in the backseat. Once we got to the Guatemalan border, they magically disappeared, and we were safe.

According to the *New York Times*, August 5: "While a worldwide television audience saw El Salvador's sunny beaches before the "Miss Universe" finals July 19, off-camera heavily armed troops were called out to halt demonstrations by students protesting the Government's expenditure of $1-million on the contest." Protests took place in Santa Ana and San Salvador. Again, from the *Times*: "According to the military Government, which contended that the march was part of a 'Communist plot', one person was killed, five wounded, and 11 arrested. But according to the students, at least 12 persons were killed, 20 wounded, and 40 arrested." Unbeknownst to us, after we left El Salvador all hell broke loose. We were lucky to get out alive!

About a month after we were back in Miami, the news kept referring to some local drug dealers as the "Black Tuna Gang," and that is when I realized Fernando was involved. Not that I was that stupid, having seen pot and cocaine all around, it was Miami and I never questioned the money he had. A few months later, Joe was found dead in the trunk of his car at the Miami Airport.

I started digging into work as a way to distance myself from Fernando. I was sure Dad would not be too pleased that he spent his money on college and got me a good job to have me blow it as the girlfriend of a major drug dealer. I wonder though, which is better, the "drug dealer's girl," or the "pimp's girl"? I think he would disown me either way.

The Black Tuna Gang was an infuriating tale of corruption, frame-ups, and media bias. Robert Platshorn, the longest-serving non-violent marijuana "criminal" to date, was the scapegoat of the failed Operation Banco, the first joint FBI/DEA operation in US history. The Black Tuna Gang was the name given to a gang led by Robert Platshorn and Robert Meinster in Miami in the 1970s. The group never called themselves the Black Tuna Gang, but the name was used by the media based on the solid gold medallion with a black tuna emblem, worn by members to identify themselves. The gang also used the words "Black Tuna" as a code when discussing drug shipments over the radio; this term was heard on DEA interception of their communications.

The gang was accused of importing around five hundred tons of marijuana into the United States over the course of 16 months. The gang operated at least at once from a suite in the Fontainebleau in Miami Beach and arranged bulk deliveries to a boathouse.

At the time, the Black Tuna Gang was alleged by the DEA to be one of the most sophisticated drug smuggling organizations around. The gang used specialized equipment to listen in on conversations by police and US Customs. They frequently used creative and unconventional methods of communication and organization, such as sending an associate a box of diapers as a coded message to signal they were ready to go ahead with a drug deal. They also modified the painted water lines on boats so they could carry larger volumes of contraband without appearing to ride low in the water.

The gang was eventually brought down by a joint FBI-DEA effort known as *Operation Banco*, which traced numerous transactions through south Florida banks until finally their accountant was caught making a large deposit in a Miami Beach bank. Also, there were informants, such as Wade Bailey of Wilmington, NC, working within the gang. The operation that exposed the Black Tuna Gang was the first joint FBI-DEA operation of its kind. Bailey was a key aspect in bringing them down. After contacting authorities, he completed a switch and carried the contraband into the Cape Fear region in exchange for immunity. Bailey later admitted that he skimmed nearly four hundred pounds of contraband and later sold it.

During the trial, certain members of the gang were additionally accused of attempting to murder the presiding judge and bribe jurors, a claim the gang members denied. One of the jurors they were accused of attempted bribery would ultimately be charged with obstruction of justice. In spite of this, a total of eight members of the gang, Platshorn and Meinster among them, were convicted and received lengthy prison sentences. Fernando was not indicted or even mentioned as a member of the Tuna Gang. It was not a coincidence that he stopped wearing the gold black tuna medallion. I was irate that he took me on his ominous ride.

I decided I would try to live my life, as best I could, incognito. It was easy to get up early and to work late and make my way home, without making my avoidance of Fernando too dramatic, although this choice had consequences as well.

"How's the love life?" Mom asked.

I was in the kitchen barely glancing at Dad's morning paper. It was like nine-thirty at night, and I was eating cold meatloaf.

"Taking a break from it."

"On purpose?"

"I'm too busy to go out during the week, and I'm kind of over the disco scene."

Mom got up and kissed me on the head. "If you wait a few hours, the news will be fresh."

"Hopefully, I'll be, too."

Mom started to leave but thought again. "I'm pretty sure, she wants to tell you herself, but with your schedule who knows when she'll get to."

"Who?"

"Your sister's getting married."

I was genuinely happy for Sheila, but I would be lying if I did not feel like I should have been first. I do not know why older siblings do that to themselves. I am sure studies show that the younger ones mature faster because they must fend for themselves more.

"I'll call her in the morning," I said.

# CHAPTER 35

My next morning left no time for a call to talk to Sheila about her wedding. The little girl, Olivia, whose mom thought our center was her twenty-four-hour drop-off zone, seemed out of sorts as soon as she got there. I did not notice it at the time, probably because she was so filthy, but she was wearing all white. Of course, her mom was unreachable, and truth be told, in the late 1970s we kept more sick kids than centers do these days. I told one of my staff members to get her a snack and keep an eye on her. Rhonda was a big woman who could hold six little ones on her lap while changing a diaper and disciplining another. I barely made it back to my office when I heard Rhonda.

"Miss Veronica, come quick."

I hurried to her room, where Olivia was in a highchair, unresponsive.

"I tried to feed her like you said, you know how she always eats like there's no tomorrow. Her head just rolled back!"

She was burning up, so Rhonda made a bath in the sink, and I took Olivia's clothes off. She had a thin red ribbon with a charm tied around her midsection, underneath her little shirt. That is when it hit me the clothes were all white and that whatever this Espiritismo shit was, it was real. I had Rhonda put her in the bath and ran to find the only person I knew who would be straight with me about what was going on: Mario. Thankfully, I was able to get his number from his mom. I explained to him what was going on. He explained that I had to find out what the mother blessed her with but in the meantime, *take off the charm and put salt in the bath.*

I had another staff member try again to track down Olivia's mother and call an ambulance while Rhonda put Olivia in the bath.

Mario showed up before the ambulance. It was the first time I had seen him in a long time. I could see that he had grown to be a somewhat shady character but underneath I could still see the frightened little boy who missed his dad. He was nervous to be there, but when Olivia's mom finally showed up, he cornered her and confronted her with the charm. I have no idea what they said, but Mario threw the charm away and yelled at her in Spanish. The ambulance showed up and little Olivia ended up being fine. Mario left with little more than a "good to see you," but I could see he was a bit overwhelmed to see that I was running this place in Little Havana.

"I owe you one," I said.

"No, you're good."

I would not say that was an everyday occurrence at the center, but it started to take its toll on me. The longer we were open, the more children found their way into the system, which was mostly subsidized by the city. Every child had a story and I wanted to help each one.

With Sheila getting married and me steering clear of Fernando and his Tuna Gang, all eyes were on me in the little free time I had at home. Mom did not come out and blame Dad but we both got the message that she thought the job was just like me helping the refugees when I was a child.

"I'm just saying, when is she going to have a life that's about her and not someone from Havana," she said.

"I heard that."

"Well it's true, you work so much, you'll never find anyone to settle down with."

"Maybe she doesn't want to settle," Dad chimed in.

"I know you don't mean what that sounds like, Den Hamilton."

"Enough," I said. "Maybe it's time I got my own place, that way you don't have to watch my life dwindle away before your eyes."

That was the first of a handful of threats for me to move out. Truth be told, I did not want to think about it. I enjoyed my parents' perspective and despite the occasional debate, I knew they trusted me. And I also knew that left to my own devices, my party side would be more than happy to take over. Living at home kept me responsible.

One night driving home from the center, I passed a slew of cop cars and blocked- off roads. When I got home, Dad was in the garage with the news on his radio.

"Police shot a motorcyclist," he said.

"I passed a huge disturbance, was wondering what it was."

"He was a Marine war vet, family man."

"He must have screwed up somehow."

"He was black. How was your day?"

"Slightly better than his, I suppose."

Dad's response hung in my head over the next few days as Miami was in an uproar over the McDuffie death. Arthur McDuffie, a black salesman and former Marine, died in December 1979 from injuries sustained at the hands of four officers trying to arrest him after a high-speed chase. The 1980 Miami riots, which were technically race riots, began in earnest on May 18, when four Dade County Public Safety Department officers were acquitted on all counts in the McDuffie murder case.

"City has an opening in fire investigations. It'd be a lateral move but could probably clear your head some," Dad said.

# CHAPTER 36

Mom was not thrilled with the idea of me going from "hell to the fire," as she said, but I trusted Dad's instincts about my life's work. He had not steered me wrong yet, and each nudge he gave me opened my world, and I would soon be at the center of his.

I made the move to work for the City of Miami's expanding Fire Prevention Bureau. This department covered everything from community fire safety education, inspections, and arson investigation, and it was made up of 99 percent men. The last 1 percent was filled by myself and another girl my age, Mercedes. Mercedes was there before me in a support staff role that she would eventually move out of and join me. That 99 percent meant it was just the two of us in a bureau of about twenty-six firefighter inspectors.

It was bittersweet leaving the Little Havana Day Care Center. I was there for almost five years, from 1975 to 1980. When I stopped and made note of that, I realized that I could easily see my life flash before my eyes there and not even notice the decades pass. That made the decision to leave easier. After I gave my notice, Carlos and I went out for drinks. We ran into Fernando, which made me uncomfortable. He and his followers were still hanging on to what was left of the disco era, and having been away from it for a while, I could see how silly it was.

I excused myself from their conversation to go to the ladies' room and wander. If I had any misgivings about leaving my job, they would soon be gone.

"She does nothing but work, taking care of other children like an immigrant maid," she said. Evidently "the voice" did not know that I had joined the Miami Fire Department.

I turned to "the voice" and was surprised to see Lourdes, my long-lost Cuban childhood friend in full gossip mode with her Cuban American friends. I had not seen her in years, so at first, I was pleasantly surprised. But then I realized that they were talking about me. I figured they were jealous that I was with Carlos and Fernando. With Lourdes, it seems no white girl could date a Cuban man. On my way back from the restroom, I locked eyes with her as I made my way back to Carlos and Fernando. Where I would normally distance myself, I made it clear to her and her friends that they were more than welcome to be seen with me. I was so glad I had made my decision to quit my daycare job and the disco scene. I was proud to be a fire inspector for the City of Miami Fire Department.

I got Fernando to get me a deal on a white Trans Am and soon I moved out of Mom and Dad's. I figured since my dad was the captain at Station 14, I would have protection from the males who did not welcome females in the fire service. I was a tomboy by day, driving my car and holding my own in the male-dominated workforce.

It was 1980 in Miami, the stuff of *Scarface* and *Miami Vice* and all the hedonistic excess and free-flowing cash that went with it. I was a certified pyrotechnician, so I worked overtime on the *Miami Vice* set mostly filmed on the Miami River. I became a member of the bomb squad. I lit up Miami as I fired each explosive. By night, Mercedes and I would poof up our hair and don our shoulder pads and go to clubs like the Mutiny in Coconut Grove where cocktail waitresses were tipped with lines of blow, and patrons lit twenty-dollar bills on fire for fun. We checked out the clubs for blocked exits, counted patrons to make sure the place adhered to the fire marshal's designated occupant load and observed behaviors that violated the City of Miami fire code. We wore earpieces so we could remain incognito when we called the bouncers to escort the violators out.

By day, we buckled up into the bureau's standard-issue uniform and went in to inspect the exact same club to charge the owner with the fire code violations. So, yeah, I was back to sinking my every moment into my work. But by now, it felt like a vacation.

My first year assigned to the Fire Prevention Bureau, Castro ordered the so-called Mariel Boatlift out of Cuba. Unlike previous tactics to get rid of those who did not serve him, the Mariel was a mass excommunication of hundreds of Cuban indigents, mentally unstable people, and convicts that he believed the US deserved more than their homeland of Cuba. The boatlift was a mass forced emigration of Cubans, who traveled from Cuba's Mariel Harbor to the United States between April 15 and October 31, 1980. The term "Marielito" is used to refer to these refugees in both Spanish and English. While the exodus was triggered by a sharp downturn in the Cuban economy, it followed on the heels of generations of Cubans who had emigrated to the United States in the preceding decades to search for political freedom and economic opportunities.

Mind you, Miami's population had more than doubled since the late 1950s when I was helping the Cubans who could afford to come to America and start a new life. Every ten years the population went up about a half a million people. What amazed me most was not that they were all coming here but that Cuba was still sending them. How many people did that island hold?

So here I was, in a new job and leading a convoy of fire service Jeeps to the Orange Bowl where tens of thousands of Boatlift immigrants were sent. They teased me that I did not know where I was going, and they thought I did not know how to drive a stick. They were dead wrong. My mind stayed focused on the convoy of National Guardsmen that was on the parallel road heading in the same direction.

At the Orange Bowl, I had to make sure things were set up safely in case of fire. I cannot imagine these immigrants were worried about what to do in a fire after being packed like sardines on a boat. But it was my first week on the job, so I kept my mouth shut and made sure there were twelve inches between each cot to conform with the NFPA (National Fire Protection Association) 101 Life Safety Code. The incoming crowd was under control; it was the existing population crowding the stadium to find relatives that made it chaos. But we managed. That is what Miami did best.

Two weeks later we were all put to the test again, when the police who shot McDuffie, and instigated the race riots in the North end were acquitted.

The once-sleepy beach community of Miami, turned host to countless immigrants, was now under fire amidst some of the worst race riots (reported) in our country's history. Just like the Mays High fiasco, I was reminded of the double standard Miami's black population lived under. How could a city that accommodated so many immigrants be racist to the blacks who are Americans and already called the place home; it could not have been a decision based on skin color. Put a Cuban on South Beach for a week, and they are darker than most any race. No, it had to be a "south" holdover. The only point farther south in the US was Key West, and that was less than five hours from Miami.

Miami burned for three days. Storefronts, homes, cars, buses, and boats, anything that could be lit on fire was torched. President Carter declared a state of emergency, and thousands more National Guardsmen were brought in. Mind you, the Cubans kept coming.

I was assigned to drive the fire service vehicle with the head inspector and police escort. There is nothing quite like driving your boss through a war zone with rifles pointing out every window. Mom joked that I was "blazing a trail to the top."

I recall getting out to assess the damage to a strip of stores. I found an appliance store still smoldering and radioed for an engine to come take care of it while the police radioed for backup to take care of the looters. The engine roared onto the scene with National Guardsmen on top. They hopped off armed with .50-caliber machine guns and charged right at us. I waved my arms so fast I thought I would finally be able to fly. I finally got them to realize I was on the good side. *Geez, I was wearing a Miami Fire Department uniform with a gold badge.* They were hyped up. I dodged many bullets that day.

"You go popping off looters, the whole state will burn," I said. Thankfully, that did not happen, but it easily could have the way the place had already turned into a war zone.

Those three days were the longest of my life, and I had a new appreciation for what my dad did for a living. Once the riots were settled, I spent the next six months dealing with the influx from the Mariel Boatlift. My team and I usually got in and out of the Orange Bowl with our heads down. We made it a point not to engage anyone, American or Cuban, or if we did it usually turned into a day-long affair that had nothing to do with our jobs.

"Veronica!" I heard it, but I kept on going. After a couple more times I finally looked for the voice. I knew it was not my team because we had walkie-talkies, but it did sound familiar. I looked over the crowd and saw Mario waving his arms.

Once we got over the surprise of seeing each other he explained he was looking for his uncle, but the Guardsmen were not being immensely helpful.

"They're treating me like I just got off the boat," he said.

I gave the checkpoint Guardsman Mario's uncle's name, and he was able to point us to the right place.

"Thank you so much." Mario hugged me and kissed me on the cheek. It brought back a rush of childhood memories. I knew he always had a secret crush on me, and we never talked about it.

"We're even," I said.

He just winked and made haste to get to his uncle.

# CHAPTER 37

The boatlift operation finally ended on October 30, the day before Halloween. The United States and Cuba came to a mutual agreement, and after six and half months, Castro had sent another 125,000 Cubans to America via Miami. Crime spiked in Miami when Castro freed the most heinous criminals from Guantanamo.

I was finally able to settle into my role and had some free time to live. Mercedes and I had bonded and started hanging out, going to the local nightclubs we inspected by day. Miami had clubs that rivaled New York. In fact, I got to know Bianca Jagger at Ménage at the Brickell Bay Club. This place was amazing. It was private and cost a week's grocery money to party for one night, but it was so worth it. My cousin from New York got the job to decorate and scored me a free membership. It was like a fantasy to step from the blue-collar life to the life of the rich and famous. We even took limos to get there because there was no parking. We never arrived until after midnight. Miami's clubs were open all night. The Omni downtown was home to Alexander's, where the dance floor was a massive glass elevator that looked out onto the street. Every night out was surreal, and we managed to get access to anywhere that was hot, exclusive, or not.

I went to New York with my cousin one weekend, and she got us into Studio 54. It was packed with scantily clad celebrities and all kinds of drugs—all the makings of a scandal but in New York it was not news. When Cher passed me with a trench coat on then opened the coat to flash her braided pubic hair, I was shocked and amazed at the same time.

In Miami, these clubs were always making news; the mob had moved in, and drugs were coming from every country south of the Keys. By the summer of '82 when Pacino was Scarface, they wouldn't even film in Miami because it was such a mess. The Florida scenes of Scarface were filmed in Fort Lauderdale. When the city got wind of how much money they lost from the film production, they vowed to make nice with filmmakers, and soon there was a deal to film *Miami Vice* there, which led to more bizarre assignments for my team: inspecting for film permits, examining pyrotechnics, measuring safe distances between actors to explosions and setting parameters to keep bystanders out of harm.

No amount of Hollywood publicity could dampen the nefarious business of drugs and mafia in Miami. One mobster was found stuffed inside an oil barrel down at the port of Miami. Shootouts were often followed by fires. I was worried for Dad.

"When are you going to retire?" I asked.

Mom laughed. "Probably when you do," she said.

"No, seriously, Miami is not the same as it was when you started, now fires come with machine guns. Every time I hear unit fourteen come over the radio, I panic."

"Don't listen to the radio," he said.

"Twenty years is a lucky run."

"Luck has nothing to do with it, some jobs come more naturally to some people."

We were in the backyard. Sheila and her family were down from Fort Lauderdale, and Dad was manning the grill. The safest time of all to broach the subject of retirement was when he was moonlighting in the other job that came naturally to him. I know Mom was playing when she brushed my question off; she was the one who put me up to it and she knew that Dad listened to me most.

He made a bet with me, that if I caught the arsonist that was making the news, he would retire. I took that bet.

As my luck and life would have it, arson was a hot governmental topic from the mid-seventies to the mid-eighties; the focus started with a 1973 report entitled *America is Burning*. This report brought attention to a crime that is largely unsolvable due to the fact that most evidence had been obliterated. The 1970s made great strides in technology, reporting, and evidence collection techniques that no doubt were partly responsible for me getting the job I did. To this day, most cases of arson are vastly under-reported in the national database.

Dad's challenge to me was the case of a restaurant fire that also put the adjacent bowling alley (that he frequented) out of commission. Being that it was a restaurant, it my immediate thought was that it was caused by a kitchen fire, so there was no real urgency in the investigation until the bowling alley owner wanted to collect on his insurance for repairs and we had to file a report.

Mercedes and I piled on the gear and trudged through the roped-off scene of the restaurant.

"Did you ever eat here?" I asked.

"Oh my God, *yes*. I loved their homemade Caesars."

"Dad always got veal Marsala, and Mom would get the chicken manicotti, then halfway through they'd trade."

"Your parents are so cute."

"I guess they are."

Mercedes looked at me sideways. She could tell I was not really paying attention, as I was knee deep in muck and inspecting all the stove and electrical appliances.

"It didn't start in the kitchen," I said.

She shined her extra-large flashlight toward what was obviously the flashpoint. "The bar."

We searched ashtrays, trashcans, all the obvious. A burned-up painting caught my eye, and I began poking around the wall it hung precariously on. There was a hidden compartment behind it, like a small safe used to be there.

"I'm thinking someone either found out the safe was missing and wanted to prove a point, or someone took the safe and needed a head start before it was reported missing," I said.

"Police report didn't say anything about this safe, just the one in the office."

We made our way to the office, which had hardly been affected by the fire, other than smoke and water damage. The floor safe was there and intact; the door was open, and the contents gone.

"Police let the owner empty it," she said.

"Looks like we need to talk to the owner, let's set a time and get them at the station."

The fire investigators in the City of Miami Fire Rescue did not need to call in the police department unless there was a homicide. We coordinated with the city police to go to the fire scene after our investigation was concluded and the scene was secure, which was fine by me. Other than the inconvenience of scheduling, I was more than happy to play it safe when it came to the mental stability of someone who set fires for fun.

The owner was an old Italian woman named Elena Accursio, her husband had passed away five years earlier, and she trusted the manager to run the day-to-day tasks. She was not planning on rebuilding; she did not even realize that she had to file an insurance claim. She thought we did that for her. We got them to call in the manager, but he could not be reached, as in he sort of disappeared. His phone was disconnected, and his apartment mailbox had over a month of mail jammed inside of it. At that point all we could do was assume he was responsible for the safe behind the painting or whatever was in its place. Mrs. Accursio was not even aware of its existence. So, in short, we had nothing other than the fact it was arson. And because it was assumed to be a kitchen fire weeks ago, the scene was more than cold. All we could do was document everything and hope the police could find the missing manager, Juan Fernandez.

"We'd have better luck if his name was John Smith in this town," Mercedes said.

That would have been that, but when Dad found out that one of his favorite restaurants and the bowling alley were ruined by arson, he wanted, "the punks punished." Now, his retirement hinged on my ability to deliver.

I cut back on going out at night and started to look up everything I could on arson cases in the past few years. We also had standard-issue dossiers that profiled typical arsonists. These were provided by the federal initiative after they started taking arson more seriously. We all knew that pyromania was a psychiatric disorder and that true cases of pyromaniacs were quite rare. Most arsonists were young, white males who came from unstable environments and were prone to substance or alcohol abuse. Which, if you can read between the lines, you see that this could be just about any testosterone laden male in the United States. But this was Miami in the mid-1980s, drug dealers, gangs, Mafia, and over a hundred thousand Cubans made up a good portion of our population, and they were just the ones that were documented. After a few weeks, I was contemplating a plea bargain with Dad. I was going to promise to keep looking, but there was no way he could put off retirement while I had to rely on Miami PD to find Juan Fernandez. It was largely out of my hands. Before I was able to get to that conversation, we had another case.

A diner two blocks from the Italian restaurant was ablaze. I grabbed Mercedes and made sure we went in as soon as it was cleared. When the news came over the radio, the dispatcher commented that it was probably a grease fire; this sort of presumption is exactly what let the other restaurant case go cold.

Mercedes and I sat in the truck waiting as the fire crew roped the scene off with tape.

"You ready?" she asked.

"Let's hang back just a few and see if anyone other than responders are taking notes," I said.

"You have been studying."

It would have been more impressive if the idea actually paid off and we spotted the guilty party watching the fire get extinguished, but we did not.

"You think someone is after all the old restaurants in town?" Mercedes asked.

"I haven't a clue, but thinking they're not isn't going to solve anything, either."

We flashed our badges and stepped through the debris. We caught up with the engine fire officer and asked if it was a grease fire. He pointed to a booth.

"Hotcakes a little too much?" Mercedes said.

"Or not enough," he answered. "'I'll be outside getting some air, looking forward to your thoughts." He grinned and left.

As we walked to the suspect lying dead on the floor, the air became sweet. It was tough to pinpoint the smells; we had wet ash, fire, and burnt food mixed with the linoleum and fake leather. But for any fire these things were not uncommon. There was something else mixed in here.

Mercedes and I both turned to each other and at once said, "pot."

It was like bricks of marijuana were the incendiaries for this blaze.

"So, we got a drug drop gone bad, but why torch the whole place?" I asked.

"Crying shame," Mercedes said.

I laughed at her. "Let's get you outside before you start eating the burnt pies."

I felt like the "pot and pie" fire, as I dubbed it, was somehow connected to the Italian place, so I did not drop the bet with Dad.

Instead, I compiled pad after pad of lists. Drug dealers, pot dealers, restaurant workers, local busts for pot, and most importantly, anyone who had a history with fire: all made the list of possibilities.

I knew the Accursio joint was not what we call a for-profit fire, at least not for her profit. Most fires started intentionally can be categorized as either for profit—where someone stands to gain from the insurance claim—or retaliation, where someone is so mad, they will stop at nothing to get revenge. Neither of these fit a serial arsonist's profile, which if my hunch was right, and the two fires were connected, that's the type of person we were dealing with: someone who is so out of sorts that their answer to every problem is to burn it.

The department was incredibly supportive in getting me any profiling help they could from DC, because of the new report and the national focus on doing better at solving our country's fires. Even so, something was gnawing at me, and I was hoping that it would not take another blaze for me to figure out what it was.

The thing was, arson inspection was only a part of our jobs, we were not like arson detectives who lived these scenarios every day, but we had to start acting like we were. And in 1985 we did not have a lot to go on, especially since Miami did not really fit a certain profile like the ones they used for the rest of the country in the federal initiative. The government had come up with a typical arsonist profile as a lone white male, eighteen to thirty-four, unhappy with their life circumstances, unhappy with relationships, and had a broken family or otherwise shitty childhood. Even today, that fits most (white) young men. Back then, it did not fit in Miami.

"You need to just let it lay, and when you least expect it, the answer will come," Mercedes said.

"You don't know my dad."

"Why don't you get your mom to talk some sense into him. Don't you think this bet is a bit much to put on you?"

Mom was the answer. I could not believe I did not think of that before. Even if she did not know the exact person, I was willing to bet Dad's retirement that she could paint a clearer profile.

Before I got to ask her, we got another call. This was a convenience store, and they saved the surveillance cam. Mercedes and I zipped to the scene. First responders found a can of sprayed lighter fluid taken from one of the store shelves.

"It can't be the same guy," I said.

"Why not? Whoever this person is, they love to be around food," Mercedes said.

"It's gotta be a dealer gone bad. He's hitting all of the drop-offs or whatever."

"It's the *whatever* we need."

If anyone had an ample supply of *whatever*, it was my mom, and she was a self-proclaimed, oft-proven psychic.

"Honey, this bet is between you and him. If he finds out I helped you he'll work until he's seventy-five out of spite."

"Seriously?"

"Seriously," Dad said as he snuck up behind us. "He's got you stumped, huh?"

"What makes you so sure it's a he?" Mom asked.

"I've lived with you and two daughters for most of my life, I serve a community of thousands, the only match a female needs to light to make a point is to the end of a cigarette and most of you still get some sap to do it for you." "You'd rather see me squirm and lose sleep than let Mom help me find this ass?"

"Not at all," he said. "I know you'll get him."

"So why don't you just put in for retirement and save me the stress?"

"Somebody has to put out these fires he's setting," Dad said.

"Wait a minute, your engine hasn't even backed up any of them."

"What direction are they moving?"

I quickly drew the map in my head of the fires. The locations were moving north. Dad's number fourteen engine was stationed in the north end of Miami.

Mom skirted past me on her way to the kitchen. "Sometimes when you live with someone for so long, they can learn a thing or two."

"I don't understand either of you."

"Sure, you do, that's why you're here," Dad said. "I don't know who is doing this, or why. But I do know that every step you have taken on your path has come along at the right time and place and served to help you on the next step. This is your job for a reason; I just thought it would be fun to spice up the challenge."

"Oh, you did, huh? I'd rather not have you sliding down that pole running head on into danger because you were feeling spicy."

Dad laughed. "I love you, too," he said.

But I was already hot under the collar, "Double or nothing; I catch this guy, you retire and you take us all, me, Mom, Sheila, the baby and even Tom, on a real vacation, outside of the Florida border."

"You're on." He gave me a big hug that I sorely needed.

I drove away and realized I was being played. The visit home did help me take a step back and relax. The answer to the arsonist question would come to me sooner or later. I tacked up a sheet of paper with basic types of arsonists alongside the basic types of crimes in Miami.

"I'm hoping if the two columns hang out long enough one of them will connect the dots," I said.

"Come hang out with me, there's a permit to inspect," Mercedes said.

Mercedes drove, which was not how we usually worked. But I was more than happy for the time to watch the streets without having to focus on them.

"If there's one thing that I'm sure hasn't changed about the Cubans here," I said. "It's that they would not risk their place of business, their livelihood, not for insurance money, not for drugs..."

"Not for nothing, but Accursio's was Italian."

"Not for anything," I said. I could not help my education degree from speaking its mind. "I know Mrs. Accursio is Italian, but she had a lot of Cuban employees."

"So?"

"So, the only thing they would risk their lives for is to get out of Cuba."

"So, we have a long-distance arsonist?"

"No, of course not, but I'm thinking it's either someone mad because they can't get their family out, or someone trying to move in and exert their authority of an area here and they're not getting cooperation."

"I guess, but in either case that person is going to be impossible to find."

Of course, she was right, but I felt like I was on to something.

We passed a film crew setting up for *Miami Vice*. We joked about delaying our inspection to hook up with Don Johnson. Mercedes pulled up to the officers on duty and asked if he was there. Turns out it was the B unit just getting some scenic shots.

"The money they spend for that show has got to be ridiculous... the cars and boats alone," Mercedes said and drove on. "It's all about drugs and prostitution."

"Also known as power and money."

As a result of streets being closed for filming, we had to go through a less than desirable part of town. Graffiti and abandoned storefronts, yes; but more so, it was what you could call the "no-to-low" rent district. The roaches here were not afraid of daylight and they were almost as big as the hair on the prostitutes that were in no danger of being busted. The cops could not be bothered to clean this block up.

"That's what I don't get. If drugs and prostitution bring so much power and money, why is all of their business in shit holes?"

Mercedes's street-smart panache was the perfect sidekick to my analytic sensibilities, and she gave me a great idea.

Carlos had been on my mind a bit lately, and I had been meaning to call him and catch up, but the arson case was consuming my every thought. It had become an obsessive thousand-piece jigsaw puzzle that I could not help but look for a piece or two every time I passed by it, whether on my desk at work or on my dining room table at home.

That night I made a point to call him, and we went out for drinks. I needed his opinion: he was the only one I could trust like family without telling my family. I had done and seen some crazy shit in my life so far, but the idea I had to push Dad into retirement was one I knew nobody in my family would go for, no matter the end-game.

Carlos was a good friend, the kind you do not see for a while, but when you do, you pick up where things left off like it was yesterday. I did not realize this, of course, until I came home from college and saw him for the first time in over ten years. After we got the obligatory Fernando drama out of the way, he wanted to catch up on more of my personal life. But it quickly veered to my work life because, let us face it, at this point I was obsessively looking for one more piece of the puzzle.

"You work too hard," he said. "I'd try and convince you to stop, but you always have, since we first met."

"That's exactly what I want to talk to you about," I said. "I have an idea, sort of a new career path if you will, one that will cure my obsession and get me a nice vacay."

"Wow, you name it. Sounds like a game changer."

I spent the next five hours and seven rum and cokes jotting notes on neighborhoods between the site of the last arson fire and points leading north that could be subject to drug dealing, gang, mafia, Cuban strongholds: you name it, we covered it. Carlos was by no means a participant in these nefarious walks of life, but he was in tune with the Cuban population: everyone from people like Fernando—his banking and Black Tuna Gang friends—to his own friends and family members struggling to make a home. He offered to ask around, but I did not want to risk one person's life for another, which is exactly what would happen if Carlos were suspected of snooping around the business of what made this arsonist go off.

That was not what Dad's retirement could be about. I had to do this myself, and Carlos led me to a guy who could point me to the arsonist. For this career move, I had to do without Dad's help. Hell, I could not even bring myself to tell him.

I told everyone I had a dentist's appointment and left the office early one day. I hurried home and traded my tomboy clothes for some smokin' eighties attire. I poofed up the hair with Aquanet and found a clingy blouse with extra-large shoulder pads. I had to laugh. I looked like I did the time I put on Brett's football uniform for a pep rally, helmet head and all.

I found Raul's place above a convenience store on a street that resembled the detour Mercedes and I had taken not long ago. As I walked up the rickety fire escape stairs, my mind went from wondering when they were last inspected to whether the homeless man below could see up my skirt.

"Why didn't I ask Mercedes to come?" I bullied myself.

I had a list of questions memorized for Raul. The last thing I wanted to do was let my guard down and refer to notes.

He spent the first ten to fifteen minutes sizing me up; finally, I asked if he wanted to frisk me for a wire. After that he backed off. But when his daughter came in and needed help with her homework, I stepped in to help. He reached for his waistband, and I stopped in my tracks. His daughter smacked him and told him that unless he knew the answer he had better back off. I helped her, and she was quickly on her way.

"Thanks," he said. "Sorry about the... thing. She gets it from her mother."

I guess he figured I was wondering where his mother was, and he said she was working. He explained that they were not married, and that she made over a thousand dollars a day as a prostitute. My jaw dropped. He laughed and commented, "you may not make that much, but you could do pretty good". He should know. He was a pimp, after all.

And that, my friends, is how I became a prostitute. It took some convincing for me to get Mercedes to be one, too. But I begged her that I needed her by my side, at least for the first few times. Then she could quit if she wanted.

I am sure you are wondering: why the leap? Before you think that all the craziness of my life and lack of real relationships sent me down a hellish rabbit hole, let me be clear: it did. But it was all in a day's work. The plan was this: Mercedes and I would go undercover as hookers in the area that we presumed would be the next place the arsonist would strike. We were not expecting to catch him while prancing around. We were just after information. Not even information from "potential customers," but from the locals who hung in the area. I had complete faith in Mercedes's ability to engage the street folk and get the word on what was going down.

# CHAPTER 38

We were not expecting an all-units blaze five minutes after hitting the streets, especially with Station 14, my dad's station.

After the building went up to in flames as the firefighters stood helplessly standing by, I collapsed, heaving in giant gasps choking on smoke. Mercedes propped me up so my bare ass would not melt on the asphalt.

"Back it up ladies," the cop said.

I heard him but it was like he was saying it from down the street. Mercedes fumbled for her ID in her boot and was able to get a paramedic to get me some air.

"No!" I wailed. "You have to go get him."

Of course, the crews would if they could. They battled the blaze for over an hour. Mercedes asked the EMT to give me something, so I would sleep. She knew I had never let them do their job. When I woke up in the back of an ambulance, parked at the scene, I panicked. Mercedes was there to calm me down.

The blaze was out, and there was nothing left of the interior. Including my father.

I stumbled to my feet and clawed at my hooker clothes. "Get me out of this shit," I cried.

Mercedes got some blankets to cover me with. A woman standing behind the crime tape threw a dress at me and I gladly put it on.

Mercedes shook me. "They have a witness who gave a description of the arsonist. She's downtown going through books."

I just shook my head like I had an affliction. "No... Mario, find Mario!" I screamed.

"Who the hell is Mario? You want me to get an officer?"

"No. I'll find him."

I did not think Mario was an arsonist, but I was willing to bet he knew who was. The problem was, I knew it was not something I could send Mercedes to take care of. I knew I was the only one he would talk to. The days that followed did not give me any time or stamina to hunt him down, so the case was getting cold. Truth be told, I no longer had a bet to save my dad's life, so the pressure had let up slightly. However, my determination increased tenfold. In honor of Dad, I was going to get the piece of crap who was doing this. First, I had to help lay my father to rest.

Dad's funeral drew hundreds. Mourners lined around the block for his memorial service. Hundreds turned out: firefighters, police, government officials, our entire neighborhood, and of course a lot of Cubans. The little girl he saved and sacrificed his safety for placed a single white rose on his casket. I felt like one of the Kennedy children, only much older.

I could not possibly take note of everyone who was there. For one, my eyes were so swollen from days of crying that I was only seeing at half capacity. The real issue was I just did not have the mental capacity to place names with faces.

But I knew a familiar voice when I heard it.

"I'm deeply sorry. If there's anything you need..." Mario said.

I spun around, and my swollen eyes nearly popped as I twisted my face so tight. "You have a lot of nerve showing up here."

"Your father meant a lot to me. I would have been in the ground long ago if it were not for his guidance when I was little."

This was most certainly true, but I did not even acknowledge it. His feeling was the least of my concern.

"I want a name or names," I said through gritted teeth.

He looked at me like I was speaking Swahili.

I had to laugh, not much, but it was long overdue.

"Imagine me in a skintight skirt, really high stiletto heels, and perfectly white, blonde bob hairdo. Never mind, forget the shoes. Now, imagine me like that in front of the apartment blaze that killed my Dad. Who do you think I saw out of the corner of my eye?"

He got what I meant and pulled me aside.

"I just need a name. I'll keep you out of it."

Mario explained that some entry-level mobsters from the northeast had been trying to establish a meth ring in Miami to overtake Cuban gangs that had just started to take root. The thugs from the northeast needed evidence as a proof of concept to their ringleaders to get their support. So, every time someone from the Cuban side heard there was a meth lab or drug zone somewhere, they would torch the building, destroying both the business and any evidence that it existed.

This was Miami's profile of an arsonist. The motives were for profit, for revenge, *and* to conceal evidence. Mario gave me the name and address of the man in charge and said, "Now we're even."

I nodded and scanned the service for a cop that I knew would handle it right away. As I hurried across the lawn collecting divots in my heels, I did a double take at Lourdes and her mother. Lourdes stepped out to stop me, but I was on a mission.

"I never thanked you for being my friend," she said.

"Sorry, I have to take care of something—we'll catch up, I'm sure."

I could not help but think how the death of someone admirable makes the consciousness of others squirm.

I handed over the information and felt the world's weight lift from my shoulders as the officer went to call it in. I turned back to the service to see the reverend give his last blessing, and tears streamed down my face once again. I felt like Dad could finally rest in peace.

As everyone filed out and arranged to go to the fire hall for a reception, I asked Mercedes if I could borrow her car. She offered to drive me wherever I needed to go, but I explained it was something I needed to do alone.

I went to the address Mario had given me and parked across the street and up a bit. Three cop cars were outside of the building. I decompressed for the first time in a long time and waited. An officer ran out and opened one unit's door, while two more struggled behind him pushing a Cuban thug—one I am sure I fitted for a cot in the Orange Bowl after the Mariel Boatlift. Thunder boomed; it was time for one of our afternoon storms in south Florida. I looked at the sky and bawled my eyes out.

It took me a long time to talk about my father's death. I cannot say I got over it. I do not think that will ever happen. I know that everyone handles grief differently, even within the same family. Our relationships are personal.

I have been asked many times if I resented Cubans because of what happened. The first time someone brought it up, I was surprised. I was never taught to stereotype anyone, and it had never occurred to me to blame the actions of a few to an entire race or nationality. If my family were of that mindset, I would have never had the experiences I grew up with. I cannot imagine growing up a white, blonde-haired, blue-eyed, pigeon-toed girl, unable to hang around with the children in my neighborhood because they weren't like me.

Honestly, if you ever meet a fireman or woman, thank them. I always knew my dad was special but after witnessing his job firsthand I found that all fire personnel are. The unfortunate events of my father's life and then death set in motion my freedom and brought me here— despite my traumatizing stint as a prostitute.

*A few years after Hurricane Andrew blew the roof off her house, Veronica finally moved out of Florida and moved to Washington, DC, where she went on to marry the Fire Marshal of the U.S. Capitol, a Fire Protection Engineer who designed the misting system to protect the book stacks at the Library of Congress and the first chemical biological detector and installed the prototype in the U.S. Capitol building. He was responsible for engineering many safety features in all the buildings on Capitol Hill. Ken Lauziere is a Fire Protection Engineer.*

*Veronica is a founding member (2003) of the Department of Homeland Security. It was formed as a result of the 9-11 terrorist attacks in the United States. In 2014, she was promoted to work as the Director of Tactical Operations for the U.S Border Patrol.*

*On to her next exciting adventure!*

# About the Author

Vicki Hamilton Lauziere is a writer from Miami, Florida. She lives in the wonderful Town of St. James in Southport, NC.

This is her first book in the Revelations Series. She is working on her second book called "Revelations in Our Nation's Capital".

Beginning in 1980, during the McDuffie race riots in Miami, she joined Miami Fire Rescue. She was a Fire Inspector, Public Information Officer, and Community Involvement Specialist as she moved up through the ranks. She was assigned the task of targeting high-risk occupancies to develop evaluation criteria with specific cognitive objectives and feedback acquisition preventing fires and injuries in the City of Miami. She responded as the Public Information Officer to fires, homicides, vehicular crashes, explosions, building collapse and any catastrophic event threatening the destruction of life and property.

Upon retiring from Miami, she joined Palm Beach Gardens Fire Rescue to coordinate Fire Service Programs in the City of Palm Beach Gardens.

In 2002, after the catastrophic 911 terrorist attacks the Department of Homeland Security hired her as a Fire Program Specialist, under FEMA to help implement the Assistance to Firefighters grant program to enhance the capability of the nation to prevent, protect against, respond to, and recover from fires, as well as, terrorist incidents involving chemical, biological, radiological, nuclear, and explosive materials (CBRNE), or other catastrophic events.

In 2015, she was transferred to the U.S. Customs and Border Protection to manage the Operation Stone Garden grant, under the US Department of Homeland Security. This federal grant program leveraged an integrated approach to address transnational criminal activity to ensure that Federal, state, local, tribal, and territorial partners established and maintained an OPSG Integrated Planning Team (IPT). She worked with USBP to provide routine monitoring and ensure that technical expertise was available to each participating agency.

Made in the USA
Las Vegas, NV
07 October 2021